Dragon's Breath

Mulau walked over to a cabinet. "I have been saving a jar of Dragon's Breath—perhaps for this." He poured two cups full of the powerful beverage and handed one to Willan.

"To long life, health, and peace," toasted Willan, touching his cup to Mulau's. "Have I missed anything?"

"To magic," replied Mulau—and downed his drink with a single swallow.

Other Swords-and-Sorcery tales
from *Ace Fantasy:*

and much more!

BOOK OF SHADOWS

JAMES KILLUS

ACE FANTASY BOOKS
NEW YORK

BOOK OF SHADOWS

An Ace Fantasy Book/published by arrangement with
the author

PRINTING HISTORY
Ace Original/September 1983

ISBN: 0-441-07069-8

Ace Fantasy Books are published by The Berkley Publishing Group,
200 Madison Avenue, New York, New York 10016
PRINTED IN THE UNITED STATES OF AMERICA

Prologue

If you were to see him thus (an impossibility, I assure you), the first thing that you would notice is the smell of incense. It is a heady scent, reminiscent of ganja and pine. Were it stronger, your head would swim.

The incense burners glow dull red. Again, were you accidentally placed upon the scene (oh impossible, impossible), you would no doubt wonder at the four braziers, with their red glow and lack of heat. For a moment, at least, would you wonder, before your eyes could pierce the fragrant haze to see the figure of a man, peering into a crystal slab.

The man is old, but his sinewy hands are strong and his face is arresting, with its painful emaciation and purpose-haunted eyes. A glance at the crystal slab would tell you why such fierce purpose is required. So, too, does the slab hint at the reasons for his gauntness and the fever brightness that hangs about him like the smoke. Great horrors are contained in the truths told by the stone.

See that sparkle there? That is an atrocity long forgotten. Observe that ripple—a treachery that may or may not occur. But these are minor truths, of no interest to anyone any more. Your attention is fixed upon the shadow that slowly moves within the crystal. The shadow is not clean dark, like the blackness that encircles the red of the bronze incense burners; no, the shadow is formed of the murky, unclean dark of an alley containing cutthroats, the dark of a coffin's interior.

James Killus

Watch the crystal closely now. Here is a small red stone, glowing foully in the dark of a murderer's pouch. There is an arch of stone, incomplete and gleaming in the mist. Beyond is a tall figure of black armor.

All of this is clear to the old man, and to you. So, finally, when you see a small golden goblet full of wine and a hand descending to drop a white powder within, you understand. The man before the slab also understands.

"Poison," the wizard murmurs. "R'Thern is in grave danger." He moves to extinguish the burners.

But suddenly, with terrible swiftness, the crystal cracks and breaks. The shadow reaches forth. It grasps the wizard, strangling him, though it has no physical form. With a choking cry, the father calls out to his son, "Willan, I am lost!" And the son hears his father die, from half a land away.

Even the gods flee such a thing. Flee now, before you yourself are snared . . .

Part One:

The Companions Meet

Chapter One

In the torch-lit darkness, before dawn:

A drum beat slowly in dirge time, underscoring the sadness of the pipes. The small procession wound its way into the hills. The blonde girl-child with the drum marched in front of the funeral pallet. The boy with the pipes, the boy with the green eyes, walked directly behind. Trailing solemnly were the elders of the clans. Sadness filled the air.

I am alone, thought Willan. *I am the last. My father is dead.* He tested the idea and could not grasp it.

It was one thing to have considered that someday his father would die. Someday, he told himself, is a mighty word. Someday, he himself would die. The House of B'ru would die also. Someday the hills would sink and the seas would rise. All was in the future, not for consideration in the present.

Yet the tapering pallet that carried the body of his father was heavy on his shoulders. He shifted his grip on the two handles that extended from the front of the pallet. As the eldest son, the principal burden was his. His brother and cousins shared the load at the sides and rear, though in truth the pallet was light enough to be easily carried by two men. Custom and honor demanded the five.

Vitor of B'ru had died of a wasting disease, it was said. Willan did not choose to dispute this. Vitor's body had been ritually desiccated in preparation for the cremation. The odor of burning human flesh is noxious; any moisture present in the body could overcome the methods employed to mitigate this unpleasantness.

The sky was faintly gray when the procession reached the crest of the hill. The sun was rising but for a time would remain hidden behind the higher hills in the east. The people of the village massed in a ring which surrounded the top of the hill, there to pay homage to Vitor of B'ru, Master of his House, leader of the Clan. The ring parted to allow the procession through, then closed again.

The bearers placed the pallet upon the pyre of dried evergreens. Bundles of bitter nitre were opened and the granules were spread in a ring about the body. Then the edge of the pallet was spread with scented oils. The air filled with the odor of pine and wildflowers. Finally, children from the village came and reverently laid dried branches upon the pyre, until the cloth-wrapped body was no longer visible.

The sky was blue by now, the sun not far from topping the highest hill to the east. Overlooking the pyre and the surrounding crowd, on a ridge between the funeral hill and the eastern hills, perched a spidery device of metal mirrors and glass lenses. Below, at the proper moment, one of the village's magicians mounted a platform and raised his arms. It was a showy gesture. The magician's critics had often chided him for his theatricalism. Still, it was not out of place; a cremation is a showy thing after all. Since the dead cannot make their sensibilities known, funeral deeds must be directed toward the tastes of the living. Simple village aesthetics demand a certain coarse drama.

The magician gave a small cry and the machine on the ridge sparkled to life. The sun's rays had reached it, though for several moments longer the lesser hill remained in shadow. A bright ring of light surrounded the pyre, just touching its outer edges. The evergreen needles popped and smoked. A flame leapt, and the pile of greenery became a fiery ring, closing swiftly. At the heart of the bright ring was an even brighter mass of light. The nitre fed the living flame which the corpse had become. There was no death smell as Vitor of B'ru was reduced to his component parts of wind and ash.

Willan, son of Vitor, last of the House of B'ru, last true magician of the Toltan race, stood watching a ceremony carried out by people ignorant of its nature. His face was wet. He told himself that he cried from the smoke of the fire. He told himself that he cried in self-pity. He did not know which was true. He remained long after everyone else had left, until morning was nearly done and the mountain birds wheeled and drifted on the currents of the sky.

Willan returned to Vitor's house. His half-brother, Jephred, was waiting there for him. The argument was quick in starting.

"I wish to leave tomorrow," said Willan. "Can you have ready for me a riding horse and a pack animal with full provisions?"

"You wish to leave?" asked Jephred in a tight voice. "But why? You have been back less than a week." The words left unsaid were accusing: *Our father's ashes are barely cold.*

"I do not know the reason," answered Willan carefully. "It has to do with Vitor's death. It is in accordance with his wishes that I go."

"How do you know this?" Jephred demanded.

"He told me just before he died."

"Vitor was alone when he died. You were still in R'tha, many leagues away."

"Nevertheless, I was with him."

Jephred's face was unbelieving. "How?"

Willan's anger broke free. "Because we were both wizards, not tricksters and showmen! We speak of magic, not conjurers' tricks performed by some village charlatan! Vitor was a full-blood Toltan, as am I. There is power in that—power enough for minds as close as father's and son's to speak without voice, even from as far away as R'tha."

Willan realized then that he had said too much. Jephred covered his hurt with anger. "So now you flee our crude superstitions to return to your new home in the great city! Which suits you more, brother—the universities of Haldor or the splendors of R'tha?"

Willan paused wearily. So many things were better left unspoken. "What can I say, Jephred? I don't much care for cities, to be truthful—but I do not belong here. These hills have absorbed all of the Toltan blood that they can hold.

"When the family B'ru settled here after the Long March those many generations ago, they were weary. They offered wisdom and craft in exchange for land and community. That exchange is complete. *You* are the heir to that bargain, Jephred, not I. I am no wiser than you. I am less able than you to live in this place. I do not belong here. I am useless here."

"There was a time when you climbed the hills better than I," Jephred replied.

"There was a time neither of us could walk. It is the people and proprieties that I do not know. My habits are uncertain, my reactions are wrong. This is no longer my home. What would you have me do? Bully my way into a position through sheer wizardry? Or should I use assassination? The repercussions would be fewer."

"You have a place in the Council of Clans. You are the head of the House of B'ru."

"The Council of the Clans is your place, not mine. As for the House of B'ru—of what use is a House with but one member? I uproot the House and place it upon my horse. It will not increase his burden. As for this house," he gestured about him. "I'm sure the Council will dispose of it wisely."

"You will not stay longer then?"

"I cannot."

"Will you return?"

"Perhaps. I am not a seer. I may visit, someday."

"You will always be welcome."

"I know. That is important. I thank you. Will you have my horse ready in the morning?"

"Yes."

Jephred, Jephred, Willan thought, *why does it have to be so hard? Why do you question me? Why do you force me to fence with the truth?*

Willan sprawled on a lounge covered with black fur in his father's study. His fingers dipped idly into a small jar of semi-precious stones. Gray pearl and jade moved between his fingers, and topaz and tourmaline. Their cold smoothness pleased him. The black furs and curtains, the red polished wood, the white and yellow metal devices sitting on shelves against the wall, swam before his unfocused gaze.

I did not tell the truth, Jephred. Forgive me for that. This is as much my home as any place can be. But there is danger for me here; danger for all if I stay. Vitor did not die of natural causes; what claimed him will find me if I stay.

What's that, you say? Who killed Vitor, you ask? Do not ask. The question itself could be your death. I do not know myself. But I will shortly. Willan's eyes focused on a small crystal globe sitting atop a pedestal on his father's desk. *I will shortly.*

Chapter Two

It was nearly midnight when Willan started up the seldom-used trail. The stars blazed with a brilliance not found in R'tha, with its smelter fog, or even in the relatively clear-aired lowlands. The distant moon glowed blue-white through the cold mountain air. Willan climbed the twisting path guided by wizard light. The light came from everywhere and nowhere and was visible only to his eyes.

In his hand was the small crystal globe.

Willan had first explored this path as a boy, playing with Jephred. They had been mystified concerning its purpose. The path led through a small canyon to a stone stairway going up the side of an unnaturally smooth cliff wall. The stairway consisted of stone slabs, cantilevered into the rock wall. It was impossible to say if the slabs had been somehow perfectly joined to the rock of the cliff or if the cliff had been carved out, leaving the steps. The steps went halfway up the cliff, then stopped.

As he climbed, the crystal sphere began to pulse and glow in his hand. The light was feeble at first, but as Willan mounted the stairs, the glow brightened, mingling with, then overpowering, the pale wizard's light. As he held the globe close to the rock face of the cliff, every bump cast a long shadow across the flat wall.

One of the bumps was directly above the edge of the last step. It cast a long black finger across the wall, directly above the abyss. As Willan moved the crystal globe, the long dark shadow touched each of three black spots, minor indentations in the wall. He raised and lowered his hand. The spots were in a line, as vertical as a stone's fall. The shadow touched the top spot, the middle, then the top spot once more. Then Willan raised the globe above his head; the shadow moved through the middle spot, lingered briefly on the bottom one, then vanished as the light within the globe went out.

It took his eyes some moments to readjust to the dimmer wizard's light. By that time the crack had already appeared in the wall. As children, he and Jephred had closely examined the wall where the opening was now appearing. There had been no cracks. But now a slab was swinging down to form another step, leaving a hole in the wall where it had been. Willan stepped upon the new step, the former side of the mountain, and stepped from it into the tunnel.

The walls of the passage gave off a pearly light, enabling Willan to relax the minor constriction of will necessary to form wizard's light. As he went forward, he heard the outer door swing quietly shut.

The tunnel was circular, perfectly so, except for the flattened floor. The walls were smooth, and gave the impression of being polished. What power had carved this passage down into the center of the mountain? He knew all that remained of Toltan sorcery. He knew nothing that could even begin this task. Willan mourned for his ancestors and their lost works.

After some minutes of walking, Willan emerged from the passageway into a large chamber. Five globes hung from the ceiling, illuminating the chamber with the same pearly radiance found in the tunnel. The globes had the same appearance as the sphere Willan held in his hand, but they were the size of melons.

In the center of the chamber, in the exact center of the pentagon formed by the crystal globes, was a large, irregular stone resting on a dais. The stone gave the appearance of an original clarity, distorted to translucence by myriad cracks and flaws. It sparkled. But the light within it was not noticeably greater than the light in the chamber.

The crystal sphere began pulsing again, the light an almost

tactile presence. Willan walked forward to the dais and placed the sphere into a small niche carved into the marble. The sphere in its niche just touched the large stone.

In the last instant before he placed it next to the stone, the crystal sphere seemed to soften in his grasp. A warm tingling remained for a time in his hand and lower arm. The pulsing light continued, growing brighter with each pulse. Willan suddenly realized that the pulses were in time with his own heartbeat, and had been so even at the hillside door.

From the sphere, light flowed into the translucent stone. Multi-colored sparks swirled within the fractures of the large stone. It was as if a door within the stone was opening, showing a world of fire and light within. The crystal globe, its work complete, dulled to darkness while the stone on the dais blazed like frozen flame.

The Oracle spoke.

"We are B'ru, who calls?"

The voice was a chorus, though it was only one voice. It was the voice of his ancestors. His father's voice was there, as was his grandfather's. There were female voices as well, voices he had never heard in life. All the voices of generations past were in that voice merged and melded.

But no, it was the voice that spoke within his head, the sound of his own thoughts.

Willan said, "I am B'ru, Willan, son of Vitor." Something made him add, "Last of the last."

"Yes . . . Willan, last of the last, son of Vitor, who was foully murdered. There is work for you to do."

Willan shivered. "What manner of work?" The answer froze his breath.

"Death work, my son, my child. An old enemy lives again. Quecora, the being who is known by men as the Demon, has returned."

The Demon. Fear accompanied that name, even after two centuries. Men shared nightmares with men long dead. A world in flames, a race destroyed, the ashes of three civilizations marked the footprints of the Demon. And cries of pain in the dead of night.

"It cannot be," Willan blurted. "The Demon was

destroyed."

"Merely driven out." The reply was curt.

"Then all is lost," said Willan.

"No. If Quecora were as powerful as he once was, it is true that no power now on Earth would even give him pause. But magic opposed is magic annulled. Quecora was shorn of his power when he was driven into . . . the place where he was driven. That power is slow in returning."

"Still, any fraction of his former power, however small, must dwarf mine!"

"So! It would appear that the house of B'ru finally has attained humility." There was an undercurrent of (self?) mockery in the voice. It continued, softer than before. "It is true that you are much less mighty than Quecora. But surely you have not forgotten how a weaker man may use his opponent's strength against him.

"Quecora did not return merely to best you in a duel. He wishes to enthrall the entire world. His power is great by present standards, but it falls short of his goal. So he uses craft and trickery to weaken the wills of men, preparing the ground for a bloody harvest. Even now, King Seilung of R'Thern lies dead, poisoned by one near to the throne, while war brews slowly in the west. This is the Demon's work, or of one willingly in the Demon's thrall. And there are other such catspaws, witting and no.

"Quecora searches for relics of the past, engines of sorcery with which to magnify his force. He wishes to reconstruct a Mindcrush or a Chaos Harp or a Death Loom. Any of these would place his goal within his reach."

A panel slid back on the dais. A dark wooden box lay within. "Your inheritance." The tone of mockery was stronger now. Perhaps mockery was preferable to the sadness which the voice was unable to keep from its next words. "We wish it could have been greater."

Willan removed the box from its resting place and opened it. Inside were three objects: a ring, a dagger in its sheath, and a gray metal wristband.

"The ring is a fire-ring," said the Oracle. "You already know something of its flame-controlling properties and its use in the curing of disease." Willan placed the ring upon his hand. The black stone flashed; it was an opal. His hand tingled for a few brief moments.

"Now don the wrist band." The bracelet was formed of two gray metal semi-cylinders hinged almost invisibly. When Willan closed the band upon his wrist, the seams vanished without a trace. The band now seemed to be solid metal firmly encircling his wrist. Again there was the tingling.

"A shadow band. It mutes spells cast at the wearer and is a defense. Also, the band is necessary in shadow walking and aids in other spells of illusion. Now the sword."

"Sword?" Willan queried, for the scabbard was hardly a hand's-length.

"The sword, D'tias," the Oracle stated. "Remove it from the scabbard."

Willan grasped the handle (a bit large for a dagger, it was true) and pulled. The touch of it against his skin was queer. When the scabbard came free, rather than a blade, there was a misty radiance below the handle. Faster than his sight could follow, the mist elongated and condensed to reveal a blade, as long as a sword, though slightly narrow. The edge seemed impossibly sharp. Moreover, the blade was very light.

"Sometimes metal stones fall from the sky. Their metal is superior to steel, especially if sharpened and made light by wizardry."

Willan, anxious to observe the reverse transformation, made to return the dagger blade to its scabbard. Suddenly, he was seized with the impression that he was holding both the long and the short blade. His eyes refused to give him fair sight. Then the blade was again encased and his memory could not tell him what had occurred. He blinked, then he strapped the blade to his side.

"These devices are ancient. They, like you, are the last of a previous greatness. They, like you, may have attributes not now apparent. Use them well, go with caution; you may add whatever other platitudes you desire."

"But," Willan asked, "what am I to do now?"

"It is unfortunate that prescience was never a strong attribute of B'ru. The way is clouded in any case. To stop

Quecora, you will require help. There is a witch of the hills in northern R'thern. Her name is Nara and she is a seer of some note. We suggest that you direct your questions to her. Also, simple observation may tell you much if you are clever. Quecora sows strife and must work through human agents to work his will. Hinder his agents and you hinder him, though you must beware thus calling down attack upon yourself. We can help you but little; you must use your own judgment at each juncture."

The voice hesitated, seeming to mirror Willan's own unease. "We sense that your path leads back to R'tha. Mayhap you will see the foundries again, if that be to your taste. There is nothing more to be said."

The voice had gone dry and whispery. "We are the B'ru that was and is no more. The dead cannot help the living. The future, such as it is or will be, is yours to make or have to lose.

"Go with love, my son."

The voice ceased. The chamber grew dark.

Chapter Three

The Demon! How to express the terror of that name? After two centuries the nightmares persisted. Nightmares of genocide, of cities obliterated, of men corrupted and societies destroyed.

Three great civilizations had existed before the Demon came: The Confluence of Nations on the northern continent, the Toltans on the southern continent and the Marek traders who habited the islands off the coast of Ismar, but who freely plied the seas. After the Demon Wars no city save R'tha remained standing. The Marek merchant navy had ceased to exist, reducing that nation's people to simple fishermen. The Confluence lay in shards, and outlaw bands held greater power than governments.

But the Toltans, the race of wizards and magicians to the south, fared worst of all, for they had borne the brunt of the Demon's might. In the end, the southern continent was rendered all but uninhabitable, pockmarked by glowing craters, racked by sandy winds and gnawed by pestilence. Some of the survivors fled south to Fire Cape, to work the hard dry land. Some reached the Marek islands, there to join the fishermen. Some undertook the March of Death up to the desert isthmus that separates North from South, ultimately to lose themselves among the southern hills and their people.

But primarily, the Toltans died.

The scars of war were everywhere, even after two hundred years. Civilization was reawakening, but it was still a fragile thing. Could it survive another war? Not again.

Dear gods, not again.

These thoughts and more were on Willan's mind as he made his way down from the hills into the meadows and pasture lands of Haldor.

It was three days before Willan reached the first town on his route. As luck would have it, it was festival time.

Festival time in a town of Haldor was splendid if compared to a hill village fair, mundane if judged against the circuses of Thile or Carnival in R'tha. As Willan walked down the street, his horse and pack ass trailing behind, he saw jugglers keeping fruits, knives and fire batons aloft; itinerant minstrels plucking out tunes for coins; magicians of the sleight-of-hand variety. Included in the latter group were some of the players in the various gaming tables that lined the street. Gambling was legal in Haldor only during festival, tempting professional gamblers to make the most of their brief license by cheating. The lack of gaming experience kept the populace naive and so made them easy prey.

A man approached Willan. "Would you care to have your fortune told? The future is my trade and craft."

"What is the cost?" Willan inquired.

"A single talen will buy dire predictions of impending doom. Two will give careful ambiguities guaranteed never to be false. Five talens will produce a glowing future for yourself and your progeny."

"What determines the price?" Willan asked.

The fortune teller shrugged. "Supply and demand. Difficulty of construction. Doom is never far removed, and so is cheap. Ambiguity is hard on the tongue. Optimism is easy but a sizable bribe is necessary in order to overcome my aversion to mendacity."

Willan smiled. "Perhaps some other time."

The fortune teller shrugged again. "A free sample then: Beware foreign entanglements." Then he turned and moved away. Willan watched him for a moment, then turned toward an ale house. His throat was dry and the trail had been dusty.

The Ox and Dragon was clean enough, though the air carried a scent of uncured wood. Some of the tables and chairs were new, built expressly for use during the festival. Willan rather liked the fresh smell. He was, however, careful to select an older chair in which to sit with his ale. He was grimy enough already, without adding resin-stained clothing to the balance.

The bustle of the street was muted in the tavern, but it was by no means absent. A dart game quietly raged in the corner. Several arguments (of a political or religious nature) proceeded less quietly at various tables. The bar maids dodged impertinent hands, though several of them, in anticipation of after-hours frolic or income, were deliberately less proficient at dodging.

Willan settled back in his chair to drink his ale and enjoy the scene.

"May I sit here, friend?" came a voice at Willan's side. "This seems to be the only vacant seat left in the house."

Willan turned to observe the newcomer and motioned him to sit. The stranger was rather short, perhaps a head shorter than Willan, but otherwise enormous. He easily outweighed Willan's slender frame by fifty pounds. His arms were as thick as Willan's thighs and he seemed to have no neck. Settling carefully into the chair (cursing softly because the chair was one of those newly constructed and was slightly sticky) the newcomer said, "I am Britar of Freeland. How fares the ale in this wood hut?"

"It is a trifle bitter to my taste, but not undrinkable."

"Ha! Good, good!" Grabbing a barmaid as she walked past, he ordered. "A tankard of ale for me and a refill for my temporary companion . . ." he looked at Willan quizzically.

"Willan of B'ru," Willan averred.

" . . . Willan, if he so desires."

Willan nodded assent.

"The bloodstones belong to Haldor," a man at the bar was saying. "There can be no reasonable dispute of this. The entire area would be lawless if not for Haldor's policing of the hills and the bandits that live there. R'thern ignored the hills until something of value was found in them and now they claim prior right. Hah! They say that we cannot protect the area. Again I say Hah! It would not surprise me if they were supplying the bandits themselves in order to harass us!"

Someone inquired about the possibility of a joint venture between Haldor and R'thern.

"Give away half of what is ours? Ridiculous, unthinkable! I'd as soon partner with the bandits and the other vermin in the hills."

A gesture made the speaker look in Willan's direction. "Well, well, who is this outlander?" he said ebulliently. He strode over to Willan's table. "A hill dweller by his garb," he continued, sniffing at the air. "And a hill dweller by his stench as well. But what is this? His belt betrays workmanship much like that worn by those in R'tha. Which are you, stranger, hill scum or R'thernian spy?"

Willan flushed but said nothing for a long moment. Just as he opened his mouth to attempt a soothing reply, Britar interrupted, "And what business is this of yours, other than as exercise for your overly loud mouth?"

The man sneered. "Ignorant *Muwars* should keep to their places."

Britar stood. "And what place might that be?" he inquired softly.

The sneer remained. "The ditch or the stable is all you're fit for, butterball," he said, mistaking the Freelander's bulk for fat.

"One so obviously high born should watch his step," Britar said pleasantly. "The rafters are low and one is likely to bump one's head!" With that he grasped the other man's arms at the elbows, jammed them flat against the man's sides and lifted. The rafters were indeed low and the man's head thudded painfully into one of them, turning his yelp of surprise into a cry of pain.

Willan yelled, "Look out!" but it was too late. One of the arguer's friends picked up a clay mug and smashed it on the top of Britar's head.

Silence now reigned, except for the sound of clay fragments hitting the floor. The back of Britar's head went scarlet, as blood trickled from a cut. He blinked and dropped the man he was holding, who stumbled and fell to the floor. Quizzically, Britar turned around to confront his attacker. The man's eyes went wide in surprise and fear at seeing his victim still standing. The entire scene remained a tableau for what seemed to Willan a very long time.

With a bellow, Britar broke the silence. Punctuating the noise was a swing that connected with the chin of the man in front of him. The unfortunate (now unconscious) man flew across the room into a group of onlookers, reducing them to a pile of tangled limbs. Two men jumped up to grab Britar's arms. He lifted them bodily off the floor and hurled them after his previous attacker. The pile in the corner accepted the two additions, the people on the bottom struggling beneath unconscious bodies. Barmaids took refuge under tables and behind the bar. Others gripped chairs as shields or weapons. The dart game continued undisturbed.

The original antagonist, the Haldorian patriot who had met the ceiling and was now on the floor, pulled a knife. He crouched and then sprang, the blade aimed at Britar's back. With a sharp yell, Willan leaped, kicking at the knife. His foot connected with the patriot's hand, and the blade sank harmlessly into a table. Rebounding from the floor, Willan smashed his knee into the knife-wielder's face.

The tavern was cramped and crowded, making swordplay impossible. Willan moved with the speed of the Toltan warrior, his feet and hands precise bursts of impact, finding knee-cap, temple or solar plexus. Britar's style was more eclectic, a mixture of Freeland militia training and street brawl. Certain tactics were clearly self-taught, such as using a table as a ram, to crush the wind from three adversaries by squeezing them against the wall. Britar laughed as he fought. His enormous strength and Willan's whiplike speed were matched against a roomful of foes, yet they held their own for long minutes. Britar laughed, a cross between a lion's roar and a braying donkey. And Willan felt his own face twist into a smile.

The end came when Willan was moving to the aid of Britar, who had five men hanging to his arms and legs and could not seem to shake them free. The bartender pulled a club from behind the bar. Willan saw it in the instant before it reached his head.

On the floor, Willan's last thoughts before lapsing into unconsciousness were of foreign entanglements and, for some reason, of darts.

Chapter Four

The cell would not have been a pleasant place even if it were clean and well lit. Illuminated by a single candle, dingy and reeking of former inhabitants drunks, for the most part, the hideous cell was tiny, cramped and windowless, save for the small vision hole in the cell door.

Willan's head ached.

"A good fight," Britar was saying. "An excellent fight. Almost worth the fine that we will no doubt have to pay. That will probably be when the festival ends. I suspect that we will have some less than sober company before the night is out."

Willan shook his head to clear it. A mistake. Through flashes of pain he asked, "Where are my ring and my. . . dagger?"

"The Sheriff took them. I doubt you'll get them back. I am truly sorry about that. Perhaps I should have been more discreet than to get into an argument with the Sheriff's brother-in-law," he said innocently.

Willan groaned; his headache was partly responsible. "He started an argument with us, as I recall."

"Perhaps he and the Sheriff share the spoils," said Britar.

Ignoring this, Willan rose and went to the door of the cell. Looking through the small barred window set at face level, he noted the door to the outer office to his left, and a large barred window across the room. The window faced an alley.

"Come here," Willan said, pointing. "Do you think that you could pull those bars from that window?"

"Probably," replied Britar after a moment's consideration. "If I could touch them. But they are out there and I am in here." He tapped the cell door. "*This* is a job for either a magician or a locksmith."

Willan smiled. "I am—both." He reached into his boot and removed a piece of stiff wire. Snaking his hand out of the window in the cell door, he inserted the wire into the lock. A moment later the door swung open. He smiled at Britar's widening eyes. "I was recently a journeyman in the metal shops of R'tha, where most locks are made. Including this one."

As the two walked to the barred window, Willan said quietly, "The Sheriff's deputy in the outer office is almost asleep. And the festival noises will mask our activities. All factors point to our immediate escape. Therefore, let us escape."

The bars proved only slightly more difficult than anticipated. They were shallowly set and with some assistance from Willan, Britar pulled one from the crumbling mortar. Then, using the first bar as a lever, he easily removed those remaining.

Crawling through the window was somewhat more difficult. The width of Britar's shoulders made it necessary for him to squirm through. "Would it not have been easier," he asked, "to have lured the guard back here and to have overpowered him?"

"Perhaps. But he might have alerted someone," Willan replied. "Moreover," he continued as he replaced the bars. "It is much better to merely vanish from our cell. They may not pursue us if we inconvenience no one by our escape."

"What of our belongings?"

"They are not here. Our horses are at the stable. My ring and sword are in a building down the street. Your valuables are probably with them. Wait here for a moment, or better still, meet me at the stable. I'll retrieve our possessions."

"But how do you know . . ." began Britar, then he stopped in amazement.

The metal band on Willan's wrist (which his captors had been unable to remove and had dismissed as worthless) became a gray glowing mist. The gray grew darker, and with it, Willan's countenance darkened shade by shade, rapidly, until his skin and clothing were midnight black. He stood at the edge of the building's shadow and wrapped a cloak (cloak? But he wore no cloak) about him. He leaped back into the shadow. There was a rippling, and he was gone.

Britar gaped. *Oh Dea,* he thought, *that's it, now I've done it. Mama always said, stay away from thieves and magicians. Brit, she said, stay away from thieves and magicians and so naturally I become a thief and fall in with a magician. You have a long life ahead of you, Brit, old boy, provided you do the exact opposite of what you are doing.*

Nevertheless, he moved down the alley toward the stable.

Britar crouched in the moonlight shadows behind the stable. The sounds of the festival reached his ears from less than a stone's toss away. A longing assailed him. Oh, for a tankard of ale and fat pockets to pick!

A shadow rippled and Willan stood beside him. "Here is your pouch and valuables. Come, our animals are inside."

"What of the stable keeper?"

"He is asleep." Britar raised an eyebrow. "He will not awaken until morning," Willan assured him.

The shorter man shrugged and followed Willan inside. The interior of the stable was very dark, but the magician seemed not to be affected by this. Britar stumbled twice, then Willan took him by the arm and guided him to one of the stalls.

"I believe this must be your horse," Willan stated. "It is the largest one here."

"Pelar?" Britar asked and was greeted by an affectionate snuffle. "What of my falcon?" he inquired.

"Falcon?" Britar heard the scowl in Willan's voice, then, "Wait a moment."

Britar fumbled in his pouch until he found a lump of sugar, which he fed to Pelar. The animal gave another happy snuffle. He patted the horse's cheek.

Willan reappeared. Britar's eyes had adjusted somewhat to the darkness, and he could make out the outline of a hooded cage in Willan's hands.

"Is this it?" Willan asked.

"Yes."

"Then saddle Pelar and let us go. I took the liberty of loading your saddle bags onto my pack animal. With any luck, our absence will not be discovered until morning. We certainly will not be followed until then, if they bother at all."

"Uh . . . I rather suspect that they will follow us," Britar said hesitantly.

"Why?"

"Not all of the contents of my pouch were there when I arrived in this town."

"Gambling?"

Britar nodded. "Some. And a certain amount of pocket picking."

Willan sighed.

The pair rode northeast, through the night and the following day. When daylight came, Britar removed Macou, the falcon, from his cage and sent him aloft as a sentry. Occasionally, Macou would swoop to attack some small bird that he had seen and would drop the bird at Pelar's feet. Britar's horse seemed inured to the practice. Otherwise, the first day's journey passed without incident, and they placed a good distance between themselves and any disgruntled gamblers, tavern brawlers or pride-stung constabulary who might pursue.

One thing, however, still bothered Willan. "If they think we are spies from R'thern, they may call a general alarm—messenger birds travel faster than we do. We had best avoid the towns; in fact, I would prefer to leave Haldor as soon as possible. This sudden enmity between Haldor and R'thern worries me."

"I," stated Britar, "am no stranger to Haldorian disapproval. Freeland threw off Haldorian domination less than fifty years ago. The defeat still rankles most Haldorians."

Willan mused, "Still, relations between Haldor and R'thern have in the past been amicable. When I left R'tha, scarcely three months ago, I had heard nothing of this matter."

"It is easy to remain friends when there is nothing to quarrel over," Britar muttered.

As long as the hills between Haldor and R'thern contained

nothing but forests and rock, easy relations between the two were assured. The forests were logged to supply wood to build ships in Thile. River transport made this possible. The river flows but one way—to Haldor away from R'thern, so there was no tension or dispute over control of the hills. Then the discovery of the bloodstones changed all that. Willan had never seen any of the stones, but he knew that they were considered desirable jewels. And he suspected they held more worth than their beauty.

They stopped to camp some time before dark; both they themselves and their animals were bone weary. They were skirting the eastern forests, working their way into the lower hills where passage was easier. Soon, they would reach the Onle river. Upon fording this stream, they would be in bandit territory, though they would be in no immediate danger.

Willan gathered scrub wood into a pile. Britar secured the horses. Macou, sensing the end of the day's travel, swooped down to alight upon Britar's shoulder. The pair conversed in little squeaking noises.

"Do you understand falcon speech?" asked Willan curiously.

Britar shook his head. "I have never heard of anyone who does. Still, Macou seems to understand what *I* say, even though it is gibberish to me in either direction. So I don't mind."

Willan smiled absently. His attention shifted to the pile of wood before him. He held out his left hand and breathed deeply, once. The black stone in his ring flashed; a fire sprang from the wood.

Macou fluttered on Britar's shoulder. "Easy, boy, I'll get your food for you now," he said. "We will worry about the safety of traveling with wizards some other time."

Later that night, Britar thought again on the subject while waiting for his overtired body to relax into sleep. He lay on his back, watching the stars through the leaves of the tree whose root he used as a pillow. *Why am I traveling with this man and why is he with me?* he mused. *For myself, I have nothing urgent to attend to. It seems as easy to continue as to stop. He is on a journey of some sort; it may lead to interest-*

ing places I have not yet seen. Besides, I owe him for my escape—not that a debt ever held me before!

But why does he continue with me? I have been nothing but trouble so far. It is my fault that we were in jail; if we are being pursued, it is due to my light fingers. What does this profit him?

Perhaps he has some task for a strong thief with a large mouth. I've heard that wizards sometimes do such things."
Britar made a face.

Who knows? Perhaps he is lonely.

Chapter Five

The thief and the wizard crossed the Onle River just after the waters had expended their fury in the rapids and white water that marked the river's escape from the hills. The Onle had not yet broadened to the width that it would attain in its passage through the forests and so was deeper and swifter than the travelers would have liked. However, their horses could swim and their bags were waterproof. They made the fording without incident.

Prior to their approach to the Onle, fearing pursuit, the pair had traveled as fast as they had dared without endangering their mounts. Now they slowed their pace, both to rest themselves and their nearly exhausted horses and because they were in no hurry to quickly penetrate into bandit territory. As a consequence of their relaxed pace, there was opportunity for conversation and questions.

Britar asked, "Where are we bound? Not that I much care," he added jovially, "but it strikes me as something that one should know."

Willan hesitated. "I am unsure as to our final destination. My immediate objective is the home of a woman named Nara, whom I have never seen. She is a witch. She lives in the hills of northern R'thern, and I am told that she has something of the power of prophecy. Perhaps she can give us information concerning the next direction to take."

Britar asked incredulously, "You actually intend to entrust your fate to some gypsy fortune teller?"

Willan smiled. "The new age dawns and scepticism flourishes. Tell me, my friend, are you a doubter full time? Are those good luck charms I noted among your possessions merely thefts which you will dispose of at the first opportunity? Some of them seem well worn. . . ."

Britar grinned sheepishly. "Eh, we all have our superstitions. My lucky pieces are small and light; they do no harm. Besides, it is not luck and magic that I doubt. I have lately seen ample proof that the latter exists, and the former haunts us all. But there is something about peering into the future that sits poorly with me."

Willan cocked his head to one side. "If I were to pick up a rock—that one for example," he said, indicating a small stone by the side of the path, "and then were I to drop it, would you feel qualms about predicting that it would hit the ground?"

Britar scowled a moment while he considered this. "The lives of men are different from the trajectories of rocks," he said at last.

"More complex," Willan replied, "and it is true that we consider ourselves capable of choice. Perhaps rocks also have philosophies that guide them in their weathering and their falls. If we but knew the language of rocks!

"However, beyond all doubt there are patterns to the workings of the world, even in the affairs of men. Perhaps it merely requires the eyes to see those patterns, and the craft to extend them into the future."

"Is that then the way prophets work their predictions? By learning the past and present and extending the pattern?" asked Britar.

Willan shrugged. "For all I know they themselves cause the events they prophesy. I merely offer an explanation to rest your mind if predestination troubles you. The ability to penetrate the future is imperfect at best. It wanes with each generation, as does all magic."

"I have heard of this before," said Britar. "I had thought it mere excuse by charlatans or the wistful longing of the nostalgic for the better times of an imagined past." He paused. "But then, I did not really believe in sorcery until recently."

Willan also was silent for a long moment, his look one of

unpleasant memory, as if reminded of a distasteful truth. "Most claims of magic now made are indeed false," he said at length. "Among the hill people a conscious effort has been made to substitute science and craft for a declining wizardry. And if the craft can be made to look magical, so much the better.

"But true magic declines. Perhaps we merely forget its application. Perhaps it is a finite quantity and is being exhausted. Perhaps not. There is an old saying, 'Magic opposed is magic anulled.' Perhaps we lose the gift through strife."

Britar said, "A drunken priest once told me of his belief that long ago one God created the universe from Chaos and Will. And then the one God split himself into many gods, who then became men. Men disagree so much among themselves, you see, that the one Will no longer holds sway. The universe has decided that it exists in and of itself. So naturally all is disorder and sorcery dies."

Willan laughed. "It is as good an explanation as any, and to my liking. I claim your priest as a relation, in spirit if not in fact!"

Between the Onle and Ma rivers lies a wedge of land given over to outlaw bands. Stretching from the forest (known variously as the Dark Forest, Thieves' Forest, and most poetically, Widow Wood) into the hills, it presents a conundrum to the traveler. The forest offers many paths, all of them dangerous, with the possibility of cutthroats dropping from any given branch. The fact that any particular branch is likely to be safe is scant comfort with so many trees to the forest. Only one unsafe one is required.

By contrast, the hills have but few trails and gaps. All have a contingent of tax assessors in the most honest form of that profession. Lucky travelers are allowed to pay a tariff. The skulls of the unlucky become goblets for decadent princes or candleholders for would-be necromancers. Such is the tide of fashion.

As the trees become brush, and before the flatlands become hills, there exists an area combining the worst features of both wood and hill. The sharpening landscape often allows but one path; large rocks and small trees allow many places of concealment. The area is called Thieves' Waste. Paradoxically, few thieves inhabit the area; there are too few travelers to make it worthwhile.

"One could hide in this area forever," said Britar, his eyes scanning the softly twisting landscape of Thieves' Waste.

Willan nodded. "King Meshed spent the latter part of his life attempting the annexation of Thieves' Forest and Thieves' Waste. It was a hopeless task, even for one as great as he."

Britar laughed rancorously. "My countrymen have a somewhat different opinion of the good King Meshed. It was he who usurped our independence in his youth, and we spent a lifetime regaining it. Indeed, we bear a mild gratitude to the eastern bandits. Without their leechlike presence, Meshed would probably have maintained his hegemony and we would still be slaves."

"You overstate your case, my friend," said Willan. "It is true that extended Haldorian dominance would be no blessing, and Meshed grew tyrannical with. Yet he did free the western states of the marauders, and opened the gates of commerce. He was a wise enough man to choose advisors who were his betters. Even now, your own common law owes much to Meshed's dictates. You had a king before his rule and now you do not. Your lot is improved. One would do well to appreciate it, unless one is certain that another path would have been more effective."

Britar replied carefully, "I would perhaps debate the question further, but Macou is flying strangely. When he flies in that double circular pattern, it generally means strangers ahead. I think . . . that we are about to be ambushed."

Cursing, Willan realized that his ring finger was tingling. *What good is a warning that stupidity ignores?* "Macou is right, and I am a fool," he said, scanning the trail ahead. "Where do you think they are?"

"Those rocks ahead are perfect crouching places," Britar said. "They are far enough ahead of that dense clump of vegetation to our left. Someone hiding in that place could block our rear, while the others attacked from the front."

"Agreed," said Willan. "I also suspect at least one archer to be up on the ridge to our right." With this, he stretched in his saddle, as if yawning, but when he finished, his bow was strung and at his horse's side.

"Does that require much practice?" asked Britar.

"Some," Willan admitted. "Though doing it surreptitiously turns out to be only slightly harder than doing it at all."

"Very well then," Britar said, "Since you have the bow, you can try for the one on the ridge and also the one behind us if you have time. If there be only one behind those rocks ahead, I will take care of him quickly and swing around to help—I hope."

"You had best look to cover in any case," said Willan. "I am a good archer, but I can be certain only of hindering the attacker on the ridge for a few moments."

Britar nodded. "At least we turn their own surprise back upon them. That is something."

It was middle afternoon; the sky was bright behind the ridge, causing Willan to squint his sly glances westward. He touched an arrow lightly with his right hand, his bow at his left.

The pair passed the clump of brush, pretending not to notice its significance. The rocks loomed ahead. Time stretched and pounded in their ears.

Something moved on the ridge.

The bandit archer stood, bow drawn, and fully exposed, sure of his safety in surprise. His dark silhouette presented a perfect target, some fifty yards distant. Willan nocked, drew bow, and let fly his arrow in a single fluid motion, but he was a little too late. The arrows crossed in mid-flight.

Perhaps the bandit's arrow was meant only as a signal and not specifically to kill. Or perhaps Willan's sudden movement had slightly startled the other archer. For whatever reason, the bandit's arrow was low, and struck Willan's horse on the flank. The horse reared and Willan, bow in hand and off balance, was unseated.

He landed on his back, his breath driven from his lungs. As he fought for consciousness, he was dimly aware of the other attackers: two in front, with swords drawn, and one emerging from behind, arrow nocked to bow, aimed for Britar's back.

Willan heard a high pitched whistle.

Weakly, the wizard extended his left hand. His ring flashed, and the threatening bow came apart in flames. Britar, sensing his chance, hurled his sword at one of his foes. The man deflected it, but was unable to do the same for the dagger which followed, taking root in an eye socket like some hideous metal flower. The other attacker could do nothing against his now disarmed opponent. Macou, in response to Britar's whistle, had swooped to buffet the man's face and to claw his eyes. The bandit dropped his sword and fled. Seeing this, the man to their rear also fled, clutching his scorched hands.

Willan gave himself to the darkness.

Chapter Six

Willan regained consciousness in a moment, though his senses were slow in returning fully. He rolled to his side and elbow, where he lay gasping for breath.

"Are you all right?" called Britar, dismounting Pelar.

Willan gave a short, sharp nod, unwilling to make the effort of speech.

Britar nodded in response and turned toward the dead outlaw. After retrieving his sword, he pulled his dagger from its grisly niche and wiped it on the bandit's shirt. Then he carefully searched the dead man's clothing.

"There is nothing here," he announced at length. "The man must have been a poor gambler. Wait here, I will check up on the ridge."

Willan waved his assent and rolled to his knees. He had not been so thoroughly winded since he had been struck both fore and aft in a game of rough-and-tumble a score of years previously. Climbing to his feet, he reflected that once every twenty years was still too often.

With soft words and deft fingers, Willan had pulled the arrow from his horse's side by the time that Britar returned. With his ring, he cauterized the wound and eliminated the possibility of infection. The ring's bright opalescence was just fading when Britar came, half running, half sliding down the slope.

Britar shouted excitedly, "By the gods, what a shot! Your arrow caught the villian squarely at the base of the throat. If

you can do that whenever you wish, you are the best bow-
man above the ground and below the sky."

Willan was about to make a disclaimer when Britar cut him
short.

"Say nothing about luck, now—I wish to believe it skill
and do not care to change opinions. In any event, see what I
found on the hapless fellow." Britar held forth his hand.
Therein lay a bright red stone of almost painful brilliance.
The light it cast rivaled that of day.

Willan's eyes widened, but Britar continued, oblivious to
the look on the taller man's face. "I propose we split the
money of sale, though it seems a shame to part with so mar-
velous a stone. It is doubtless one of the bloodstones of which
we have heard! Perhaps. . ."

"Drop it!"

"Eh?" came Britar's startled reply.

"Drop it, I said!" commanded Willan, D'tias now at full
length in his hand.

"Here, now," gulped Britar, backing up. "I . . ."

Willan swung D'tias, striking Britar's hand with the flat.
The burly man gave a yelp and the stone went flying. After a
second's recovery, Britar drew sword and prepared to defend
himself, but to his surprise, Willan no longer confronted him.
Instead, the tall wizard had taken several steps toward the
fallen bloodstone, and now stood silent. His knees were
slightly bent, and he held his sword loosely, pointed at the
gem in the attitude of duel.

"What do you . . . ?" began Britar.

"Quiet!" Willan rasped, his attention fixed upon the stone.

Suddenly, from D'tias came a pale blue flame, which
leaped the two-yard gap between swordtip and stone, engulf-
ing the gem in brilliance. In response, the bloodstone was surrounded by a red aura, brighter in hue even than the stone
itself. The beauty of that aura hurt their eyes. Yet it seemed a
splendor unclean, as the glowing eyes of an opium user are
beautiful.

The aura throbbed, but it became clear after several seconds that it was waning. Finally, after nearly a minute, the
flame touched the stone. A loud snapping sound and the

stone split into three colorless fragments, the terrifying beauty vanquished.

After some moments, Britar asked, "What did you do?"

Willan answered, "I do not know."

"Well, then, why did you do it?" rejoined Britar.

Willan touched his forehead where sweat had beaded on his brow. His voice was thin and distant.

"Two centuries ago," he said, "they were not called bloodstones, but rather Devil Gems. Quecora, the Demon, often used them in payment for services that traitorous humans rendered him. The gems attack the will as surely as any drug. They steal the soul through greed and lust for beauty. So pretty they are, so pretty. . ." He stopped for a moment, then resumed. "Had you remained holding that evil rock for an hour, you would have decided that it should not be sold. Within a day, you would have been trying to buy back the half that you so generously gave to me. Within a week, you would have killed me for it." He smiled a wintry smile. "Now we know why Haldor and R'thern are ready to war. Quecora is inspired in his scheming."

Britar scowled. "The Demon War ended two hundred years ago. The Demon was killed, was he not? How can . . . ?" His voice trailed off.

Willan sighed. "I'm sorry, Britar. I should have told you earlier. I did not because . . . well, I did not." He grimaced. "But I must tell you now. Quecora, the one called Demon, is not dead and he has returned. My purpose is to find a way to stop him if such a thing be possible."

Britar looked from Willan to the three clear shards on the ground, then back. Slowly, as the sense of the other's words grew, he sank cross-legged to the ground, as though crushed by the enormity of those words.

"Oh me," was all he said, turning his head from side to side. "Oh me."

Dionel, protector of minstrels and thieves . . . No, that won't work, I have not believed those superstitions in years. O Dea, mother of heaven and earth. O Braal, lord of . . . No, No! No.

Mother of an Anollonian dog, I must pray to something! I shall never get out of this by myself.

O Britar, master of stupidity, father of bad luck . . .

Desist!

If I do not accompany this wizard bent on suicide, I must hide. But what place on earth is safe from the Demon? I have seen tumbled ruins where he stepped, and fields where the flowers still refuse to grow. To hide and wait for the stone to fall . . . such a notion sticks in the throat. Yet, to seek him out, to throw oneself into the storm—do I trade a sniveling death for an early one?

Am I a free man or a common thief? What would a thief do? Run, of course. But a free man is free. Free to . . . to . . .

To do what?

To suffer indecision, by my ears! Characters of heroic tales suffer no such malady. They never falter. And they never die until the tale is done. But which of us is this tale's hero and which merely the friend? Friends of heroes do die. Am I a friend of the wizard hero or is he a friend of the heroic scoundrel?

Or is the Demon writing this tale for his own amusement?

After many long minutes of silence, Britar sighed and said, "In the village of my birth, there was a boy who was always doing outlandish feats of skill and bravery, such as climbing Mount Aramo, or swimming Deepsea Channel. He was not very bright, I fear, and it was the others, the ones with less courage and more sense, who conceived his undertakings. I once asked him if it were not foolish to rise to every challenge laid before him. He said, 'I am not clever enough to think of interesting and manly things to do. So I follow the suggesions of others. This way, my life is more full and I am a better man than I might otherwise be.'

"He is probably dead by now, poor fellow. I have not been back in years, so I have no way of knowing. But I never believed that his life would be long. Merely full. He was successful in that I am sure."

He reached for the reins of his horse. "Come," Britar said. "We must go. Still targets are the easiest; at the very least let us be difficult targets."

Chapter Seven

The pair rode hard, eager to be rid of Thieves' Waste. Had the passage sufficient flow to support more than one group of bandits, they would surely have fallen prey. Their pace was too quick for good defense. But they had developed a revulsion for the area. It reeked of sour magic.

They rode north, crossing the Ma River, and passing within sight of the verdant fields of northern Haldor. Soon they reached the road of Imam, crossed it also and turned eastward, parallel to the thoroughfare. They then skirted several companies of Haldorian troops, who were camped along the road, building fortifications. "I smell war," Britar muttered and Willan nodded.

The military activity increased as the pair moved east, forcing them to turn north well before Haldor Pass. Their rate of travel now slowed, as they picked their way into the jamble of scruffy hills that lay in front of them. The sense of immediate doom engendered by the episode of the bloodstone had retreated, leaving only a residue of gray unease. The two said little as they made their way into the wind smoothed landscape that crouched beneath a lowery sky.

It was that indeterminate season between dry and wet in the hills. Though the clouds hung low and gray, the rain came only in grudging little patches of drizzle, and the grass still grew brown instead of green. The weather seemed dedicated to discomfort rather than hindrance. While Britar profaned it for bastardy—it being neither sun nor rain—he saved his stronger curses, knowing that they would have use when the rains came full measure.

Then, unaccountably, the weather reversed itself and dispelled the clouds, banishing them to the horizon where they gathered in preparation for the storms to come. The two travelers rode in sunlight beneath a clear blue sky, and came in time to the home of Nara, witch of the Northern Hills.

It was a simple house, indeed, a mere cottage set between two tall trees. Britar was surprised when informed that this was their destination. Still, he thought to himself, what did he expect? Unpainted shutters and creaking hinges? Did he expect towering spires and flashing turrets? True magic, he supposed, would have little need for theatrical tricks and atmosphere.

It was then that he took notice of the lawn of green when all else was brown, and the bed of flowers giving strange shapes to colors just slightly unlike any that he had seen before.

They dismounted and made their way to the door. Willan raised his hand to knock, but the door swung inward before his fist could strike.

"Who are ye, and what do ye want?" said Nara.

She was tall and brown, nearly as tall as Willan, with skin a rich walnut hue. Her hair was short cropped, in the manner of the gypsies, and was several shades lighter than her skin. Britar would later notice that her eyes varied with lighting and mood from golden tan to mahogany. Now they were midway in color between her skin and hair. She was youthful in appearance but of unguessable age, and though her face was strong and without blemish, she might have been considered ugly to some. Surely she would be beautiful to others.

Willan blinked at the greeting, stammered a moment, blinked again. Then he smiled wryly. "You are a teller of fortunes, I believe. Should you not be expecting us?"

Annoyance flashed in her face. "It is ye, all right," she said. She seemed to be considering slamming the door in their faces. Instead, she flung it wide. "Well, I suppose ye must come in. I've known for a time that bad luck was coming, but I did not expect ye today. I've not tossed the coins or the cards for many days." She seemed to be talking to herself as much as to the men before her. She beckoned them to enter.

The interior of the cottage gave the impression of space, of being much larger than could be contained by the exterior. This effect was not due to any arcane practice or black art; a profusion of mirrors was responsible. They lined the walls in resplendent variety. Some had textured surfaces. Some were set in ornamental frames. The multiplicity of images was at first confusing. Then, as their senses adjusted, Britar and Willan marveled at the brilliant simplicity of the decoration. A single candle could illuminate the entire dwelling, the light extended by reflection upon reflection. In the daylight which entered through windows of various geometry, the interior of the cottage dazzled the eyes.

Later in their acquaintance with the prophetess and witch, Britar would realize that the cottage decoration had served other purposes. When removed from her home of reflections Nara showed the habit of nervously glancing over her shoulder.

Nara gestured them to chairs and they seated themselves around a table. Once seated, Willan began to speak.

"Our purpose concerns. . ."

"Shush!" Nara exclaimed. "Any fool can tell a fortune already known. First tea, then I will toss the coins. I'll not be hurried."

As if to counter her own words, she arose and began to rush about, gathering cups, saucers, bowls of loose tea and other spices to place before them upon the table. This task accomplished, she went to the fireplace and lifted a heavy kettle from its place above the fire. Britar nearly volunteered aid, but thought the better of it.

With the tea poured and having supplied her guests with sweetmeats and pastries containing dried fruit, Nara closed the shutters of the cottage windows, thus muting the light that had filled the room. She then seated herself at the table. "Now to business," she said.

Reaching into a pouch that hung from the table, she produced five bronze coins, ancient in appearance. After shaking them in her hands she slapped them onto the table.

All five coins presented the same side, the laurel and cross.

Nara scowled and pursed her lips. She picked up the coins and repeated the procedure, shaking the coins more thoroughly and slapping them to the table with a savage gesture.

Again the five coins showed the same side, but this time the coins presented the four-horned circle, the obverse of the former trial.

She shook her head slightly and performed the act once more.

The coins repeated their initial performance. Five laurels and five crosses stared up at the waiting trio.

Her brow now deeply furrowed, Nara returned the coins to her pouch and removed a pack of cards. She shuffled them nimbly with well-formed and supple hands. Then she dealt out a complicated pattern, face down. She reached to the center card and turned it.

It was blank white.

Nara drew a deep breath, bunched the cards into a pile once more, shuffled and redealt. Again she turned the center card.

This card was also blank, but this time its color was jet black.

For a long moment, she was quite still; only her eyes moved from the cards to Willan and back again. Then she muttered something under her breath.

She rose and walked to a broom closet. From the closet she removed a heavy staff. Its head was ornately carved and dark. Down the length of the shaft the wood grew lighter until it was nearly white. The tip gave the appearance of blond ashwood, the head of dark mahogany, though the grain ran unbroken from the tip to head.

"Ye know wizard speech," she said to Willan, half as a question and half as a statement.

Willan nodded.

"Rise and take my hand. We may work the quicker this way." Nara extended her hand toward Willan.

Willan rose and took her right hand in his. Nara grasped her staff and struck it once upon the floor. Their eyes met and all movement ceased.

The tableau remained unchanged before Britar's wondering eyes for many minutes till he arose and began impatiently to pace the room. His pacing took him to a door which he took to lead to a bedchamber. Out of curiosity he placed his hand to it and pushed. It did not move, nor even rattle, as might a locked door; it was solid as a wall. He turned and strode to the other end of the room. Here, the pantry door stood before him, slightly ajar. He opened it and studied the shelves of food therein. The pantry was well stocked and the rich food smells teased his appetite. He returned to the table and consumed several more pastries.

Outside, a wind was rising.

He moved to a hexagonal window and opened the shutter. The wind caught it and tore it from his grasp, slamming it against the side of the house. The sudden movement and noise startled him. Yet when he turned, Nara and Willan were still frozen, eyes locked, their breathing in unison.

"Transfixed, they are," Britar said out loud, partly to calm himself with the sound of his own voice. "I hope they soon return from wherever they have gone. The storm will hit and our horses need shelter from the wind and rain. Hmmm. Now there is a thought."

After first closing and securing the shutter that he had opened, Britar exited the cottage. The wind had turned to whipping fury and he had to shield his face from blowing dust. Just to the northwest rising far above the hills a thunderhead towered vast and angry. Britar shivered, not altogether from the chill.

"Here Pelar, easy . . . easy." He saw that Macou had alighted and entered his protective cage. No flying weather this. He reached for Pelar's bridle. The large horse shied and flipped his head away.

"Now, now, let us have none of that," he said and reached again for his horse's reins. Again Pelar sprang back, and this time Willan's horse also gave a snort and seemed ready to rear.

"What the . . ." Britar began, but was cut short by a lightning flash and a clap of thunder close on its heels.

This time both horses did rear and the pack animal bucked

as if to toss its burdens. These were securely tied, but Macou's cage came loose from Pelar's back and Britar barely managed to catch it before it struck ground.

A dread now seized him as the darkness increased, bringing nightfall to midday. The growl of thunder grew and mingled with the frightened cries of the horses. Retreating from the animals, Britar slipped and fell heavily to the ground. Macou shrieked his displeasure.

Britar scrambled to his feet and picked up Macou's cage. Choosing his steps with care, for the world seemed to present a slight tilt to his vision, he hurried to the cottage door, flung it wide and entered. The terrified clamor of the horses followed him inside.

The room seemed filled with a curious mist. Britar set the cage upon the table and rubbed his eyes to clear them. The mist remained.

"Willan!" he said loudly. "Nara!" he shouted, to no avail. The pair remained transfixed.

It seemed to Britar that he heard a tangled chorus of voices, all jabbering in chaotic rhetoric. Some were high pitched and shrill; some were low and guttural. Others blended with a ringing in his ears.

"Willan! Nara!" he again yelled at the oblivious pair. "This storm! It grows too fast! There is. . ." He reached to touch Willan's arm.

Britar screamed.

Chapter Eight

In the moment that Britar touched Willan's arm it seemed to him that there appeared a rent in time, a vast cavern into which he fell headlong. It was a fearful descent and endless. Each succeeding instant was the instant before he crashed from a great height. Each moment stretched for longer than a lifetime. Voices screeched insanely in his ears. Talons ripped at his flesh. All he loved was false. All the world was evil. It was every nightmare come true. It was madness. It was death.

He screamed. He screamed until he thought his lungs would burst. He screamed until he thought the sound of it would pierce his own ears.

For a brief instant the cottage scene reappeared before his eyes. His hand was still on Willan's arm. All pain radiated from that juncture, yet he could not release his grasp. Instinctively, in panic and hysteria, he swung his other hand with all his strength, striking Willan's chest with open palm. The force of the blow sent Willan sprawling stiffly across the room, reflexes substituting for volition. The connection that linked the trio broke and Britar screamed again. Red darkness descended upon him as pain blotted out his wits. When his senses returned, Willan and Nara were helping him to his feet.

"We must flee!" yelled Willan above the thunder. The storm outside shrieked and pounded at the house. The windows were open; several of the shutters had shattered or were

43

hanging by a single hinge. The wind whipped through the cottage as though trying to steal their breath or snatch the words from their mouths. The lightning came with such nearness and regularity that the thunder was continuous. The radiance that filled the room pained the eye.

"Macou!" croaked Britar as he tried to straighten his legs. But he saw the door of the cage swinging freely. The falcon was no longer within the cottage.

"There is no time!" yelled Willan. "Can you . . . ?"

"Get down!" Nara screamed and pushed at the two men. There was an explosion of lightning just outside the window and a large tree limb came smashing into the cottage roof. Bits of slate and wood rained down from the hole that appeared above them.

"Now, run!" yelled Nara. "Get to the ditch that runs in front of the house!" Britar looked wildly about, trying to see through the curtains of rain. There lay the ditch, a hundred yards away. Britar ran awkwardly, his left arm numb and useless, his feet slipping in the mud. Willan held him by the waist, trying to hurry the pace.

When they reached the ditch, Britar had a moment of dismay. The trench was wet with rivulets of muddy rainwater. Could one drown in this ditch? he wondered. Then still another lightning flash and clap of thunder came from behind them and he threw himself forward into the mud. The darkness again claimed his soul.

Britar awoke slowly.

He was lying on his side in the ditch, his ear in the mud. He tried to feel the foolishness of his position, but he lacked the strength. His arm was folded under him. It was no longer numb; instead, it hurt as if he had been stirring boiling water with it. He rolled over onto his back, wincing at the pain.

The storm had departed, leaving only a light rain. Britar let the drizzle wash the mud from his face and hair as he gathered his wits. Macou fluttered down to the ground beside him and made an irritated noise. At the sight of the falcon, Britar felt his spirits rise a little.

Willan appeared over the lip of the trench. He carried firewood in his arms. Dumping it to the ground he turned to crouch by Britar's supine form. "How are you?" he inquired.

"Amazed, I think," answered Britar. "My left arm is still with me. I seem to have a memory of it being ripped loose with red hot pincers."

"Um," grunted Willan. "Let me see it." Taking Britar's arm in his hands, he traced the muscles and nerves with his fingers. The stone in Willan's ring glowed with a golden softness as a warmth spread through Britar's arm. The band on Willan's wrist also reflected a soft golden light. The sensation of having been scalded began to wane as did the soreness of his muscles, a soreness which had seemed to penetrate the bone.

"What happened to us?" Britar asked.

"We stumbled into a trap, I think," Willan said. "I do not believe that our antagonist still retains the command of the elements. Too great a power is required. But we reached for knowledge that has lain dormant for centuries. I suspect that we tripped a snare that Quecora established in his first visitation. We ran afoul of a sorcerous remnant of the Demon War. Nara and I both knew of the prohibitions surrounding knowledge of the Demon but we discounted them as mostly superstition. I was the greater fool. My father died while tapping such knowledge. I should have better realized the danger. We thought that foreknowledge and caution would suffice as our protection. We were wrong."

"Where is Nara?"

"She has gone to recover our horses. She should return shortly."

"How long was I unconscious?"

"Perhaps an hour," Willan replied. "I should tell you that you saved our lives, and possibly your own. If you had not separated us at the proper time, we would have perished in the storm. The ultimate fury of the elements was muted by our escape. The storm ceased to grow when we threw off our transfixion and fled the house."

"The storm could have been worse?" There was a tinge of hysteria in Britar's voice.

"At his height Quecora turned a continent to ashen slag. We battle dim reflections of that power, yet still we must walk with desperate caution. I do not dissemble. I fear our enemy more than death."

Britar grimaced and shook his head as if to toss away the memory of his recent pain. "Fine," he said. "But please avoid such total candor for a while. I think perhaps that I have had my fill of truth today."

For several moments the pair gazed off into the drizzle, each thinking private thoughts. Then suddenly there came a cry from behind them, not loud but with the sound of anguish. They scrambled from the ditch to find its source.

When she went to find the animals, Nara had avoided looking in the direction of her house, her home. She had felt its pain and agony during the storm and she had smelled the fire when the lightning had struck. She had heard her dwelling die. She dreaded the moment when she must look upon the corpse. So she fixed her concentration upon the task at hand. First to find the horses and the pack animal. Then return. Then . . . do not think of that. She refused to cast her sight into the future for fear of what she would see.

And yet, when she returned, staff in hand, the animals trailing behind her, determination failed. The scene burst upon her too suddenly for her resolve and it overwhelmed her senses.

A splintered tree limb lay across the cottage like a wrathful fist. One wall had collapsed under the weight of the limb. Another wall had burned and fallen inward. Only a few drops of rain continued to fall. They sizzled as they touched the few remaining embers on the side of the cottage which had burned and fallen.

She knew that inside the fire had been worse, with no rain to quench it save that which dripped through the smashed roof. Her mirrors would be black and broken in their frames. They would lie smashed upon the floor. Their fragments would have joined the litter of smashed slate from the roof, the ashes from the burned walls and rafters, the charred remains of her furniture.

Nara the gypsy stood before the only home that she had ever known. The constancy that she had built with such pride and care lay in ruins. She stared at the wreckage with a sight that pierced the fabric of time. She knew the future of the battered shell before her. It had no future. Her figure and countenance were rigid as she gazed into the void. Then her pain broke unbidden from her throat and she cried out.

After a moment the tall one and his bulky friend came to the scene. They approached her timidly, the one called Willan more reluctant than the other. The wizard had touched her mind in the time before the storm. Perhaps he knew something of her mood. She did not care. She felt herself grow numb.

Britar broke the silence. "May we be of aid?"

Fury flared in her, washing away the ice. "Ye can go! Be on yer mounts and to the pit with ye!" She raised her staff and seemed about to strike the startled thief. Instead she whirled and swung the staff in a wide arc. Its dark wooden head struck the corner of the cottage with a sickening *crunch.* The corner beam broke and split in two. The wall sagged lower. The two men stared in shock.

"What are ye looking at!" she yelled. "I built this house. It was my home. Mine. *Mine!* Do ye hear? I raised its beams; I fed its strength and it sheltered me." She swung again and a section of the wall exploded inward. The house shuddered. "Now it is dead. I am homeless again. But I will *not* leave behind a senseless hulk. I raised my home from the nothingness; to nothingness I'll return it." She stamped the staff next to her foot and a thin flame leapt to rekindle the fallen tree branch. She swung again and an overhead beam splintered and collapsed.

She whirled again to confront the two onlookers. "Are ye still here? Are ye deaf? Leave me! Let me attend to my task alone!" She closed her eyes and breathed a silent sigh. A moment passed, filled only with the sound of rising flames. Then she said quietly, in a different voice, "Return when I've finished if ye must. I know ye must. I've not forgotten the task before us. But leave me for a while. I must complete the cycle and it's a private thing." Then she turned her back.

The wizard and the thief left her then, leading their horses to the ditch where the firewood lay waiting. They would make a warming fire to dispell the chill which the cottage fire only seemed to increase. Only once did Britar turn back to look at the silhouette of the gypsy witch against the dull red light of the mounting flames. She stood motionless, an ebony statue poised at the lip of hell.

Two men sat in a ditch.

The rain had begun again, not hard, but with enough vigor to threaten the small fire which Willan tended. From time to time he would lean closer to the fire, his arm outstretched. His ring caught the light of the fire and sparkled. The reflection grew brighter; the fire leaped to greater activity, dispelling the rain.

From behind them there came a sharp *crack* and then a crashing of rock and wood. "What was that?" inquired Britar.

"I believe," said Willan without bothering to get up to peer over the side of the ditch, "that Nara has just destroyed the chimney of her house." Several bursts of crunching and grinding noises punctuated his words.

The two men stared into the fire as the sounds of destruction and dissolution continued. The flames induced a revery. The shadows danced at the edge of the darkness.

"This cannot be real," said Britar.

Willan raised an eyebrow.

"Here we sit in the rain warming ourselves by the fire," Britar continued. "The fire was constructed of damp wood. Damp, did I say? It was soaking wet, waterlogged. It should not burn, even if thrust into an already blazing fire. Yet your ring merely strikes light and the fire burns merrily. It speaks to the wood in fire talk, I suppose. Your ring could burn rock."

"Certain kinds of rock," Willan admitted. "They are relatively uncommon, if that helps."

"Not in the slightest," Britar said. He glanced over his shoulder toward the unseen destruction nearby. "Behind us a gypsy is destroying her house. Gypsies do not live in houses. They travel about telling fortunes, running games of chance and other swindles. Yet this one had a house which to all appearances she loved beyond all else. But she lost it in a storm which arose by magic because the two of you asked some over-delicate questions. Now she completes its destruction, wielding a wooden stick which smashes stone. She threatened me with it earlier. Had she struck me with it I would now be a pulp."

"I did not expect such power," said Willan. "I see why the oracle sent me to her. She is capable of many surprises. That will help us greatly."

"Oh yes," said Britar. "Oracles. Second sight, prophesy, quests, magic swords, devil gems, demons and sorcery. Intrigue. Damnation. Death. This cannot be real. I have stumbled into a madman's dream."

Willan looked at his friend. "Listen," he said. "Perhaps all of this is the joke of a god or the dream of a madman. That does not matter. It is all we have and so it is real. I am real; you are real; Nara is real. The rain is wet, the fire is hot, and an injury will hurt with very real pain. I have lost a father and a heritage as part of this game. Nara has lost as much or more than I. You yourself have seen hell from the inside and you wish to deny it. Very well, deny or forget, it is all the same. But do not slacken or waver. Do not lose courage or determination, even if conviction fails. We cannot afford it. We walk the edge of the pit. Remember that, if nothing else. *You can die from this game.* Death is as real as life, and it is much more permanent. Fantasy or no, we must succeed in our task. The alternative is unthinkable. We must not fail. *We must not fail!*"

Britar accepted these words impassively. He stared into Willan's face for a long time, trying to penetrate to the soul of this man who had yanked his life onto such a fearful path. He had known the magician for only a few scant days. Yet he could barely conceive of the time before their meeting. He shivered, not altogether from the cold and damp.

"I understand," he said. "I accept." Then there was nothing more to be said. The two men waited for the dawn.

They returned to her in the morning. They found her kneeling on the ground, her hair hidden beneath a scarf. She tossed the coins onto a bed of crumbled rock and mortar.

"It is one of the oldest forms of divination," she said, her voice low and even. "One tosses the coins. The answer comes. One ponders the answer until the question presents itself." She picked up the coins and tossed them again. She touched their shining faces where they lay. "The answers are all the same. Death and transfiguration. The wheel turns; we are dust. The questions make me tremble."

She scooped up the coins and rose to her feet. "Come," she said. "All things revolve around the Beast. We must strike the chord, cut straight to the center. Only at the center may all paths be seen." She shook herself and took a step.

"R'tha," she said.

Part Two:

The Carnival City

Chapter Nine

On the first day of their journey to R'tha, the travelers spoke little. The camaraderie between the two men had been punctured by the recent disasters. The presence of the gypsy added to their discomfort. While the men rode in awkward silence, Nara brooded. It was clear that she still mourned her loss and she had begun the signs of some other, hidden strain. Her occasional nervous backward glances gave evidence of an underlying tension not altogether explicable by the awful nature of the task before them. Britar found himself remembering the room of mirrors.

At Britar's suggestion, the gypsy shared Pelar's broad back. At the first opportunity they would acquire a mount for her. Until then, her additional weight made little difference to the large animal. A horse accustomed to Britar's weight would barely notice so small an added burden.

Once only during that day's ride did Britar attempt to breach the silence. He cleared his throat, then asked, "By what name do the gypsies call themselves?"

"Yani," she replied and then said no more.

So much for polite conversation, he thought and gave himself back to his private hush.

When the day's travel was done, it was Macou who finally broke through the ill humor. Sunset came early in this part of the hills, and the trio stopped to make camp by a small stream. While the shadows grew, Willan made a fire. Britar filled a goatskin pouch with water from the stream.

The pouch had been slit down the middle. When placed upon a proper arrangement of rocks it formed a shallow trough. On seeing the goatskin wrapped pool, Macou gave a happy cry and alighted beside the water. After first drinking several swallows the falcon hopped into the shallow pool and began to clean himself. The joyous splashings of the bird caught Nara's attention. She leaned against her staff for several minutes while she observed the spectacle. A smile slowly spread across her face. At length she chuckled.

"That is a male bird, is it not?" she asked. "I had thought that all hunting fowl were female."

"Generally that is true," said Britar. "But Macou is a very unusual creature."

"Where did you get him? He is of a species unfamiliar to me."

"And to me also," Britar answered. "I have never seen another like him. He is a true falcon, that much is clear from his beak and nostrils. His markings are somewhat similar to the kestrel. Note the light bars of black upon the brown. Yet he is as large as the female peregrine and his head is larger still. His origins are most perplexing and I would not trade him for a flock of eagles.

"I acquired Macou in Dree several years ago. For various reasons—mostly involving gambling debts—I found myself indentured to Lasmir Du, chieftain of one of the many factions that abound in Dree. It was easy work. My principle duties were to instruct and train his sons in certain of the military arts. My own expertise in such matters is desultory, I admit, but it sufficed to impress the chief. As a minor duty I was to also oversee some of his hunting enterprises. He had a large kennel—large at least for Dree—and as in all of Dree his horses were of the highest blood and training.

"From somewhere they had heard of falconry. The tales that reached their ears were, I suspect, vague, but imaginations were inflamed. The only birds of prey in Dree are found in the place of the Stone Fingers, tall spires of rock that are nearly impossible to scale; but someone did climb high enough to capture several birds, among them Macou. I hesitate to imagine how many men died before the successful attempt was finally made. Dreemen are not climbers; they are accustomed to gently rolling countryside. They prefer horses to their own feet in any event. Still, they are proud, and if their chief says climb, by God, they will climb rather than admit to fear.

"The training of the 'falcons' had been left to a nephew of the chief, one Korik by name. In fact, most of the birds were not true falcons. There were several hawks and even what seemed to me to be a species of vulture. But these lesser fowl had responded to such rudimentary training as Korik could provide. He began with little and accomplished little; I could not judge him harshly for that.

"But Macou . . . oh, what he had been doing to Macou! Unable to control the finest of his flock, Korik was attempting to starve Macou into submission. It is a tactic that will work, given time, but it forever ruins the bird to which it is applied. Such abuse smashes the spirit when patient molding is required. Such a thing is abominable!"

Britar paused. A look of contrition flashed upon his face. "I lost my temper, I fear. Korik was an unintelligent insensitive clod, but these were hardly traits uncommon in Dree. I picked him up and threw him down a well. Several of his friends saw, and laughed. So I made an enemy. Some months later, after I had thought the matter finished, Korik conspired to have me blamed for a theft. Lasmir Du realized my innocence but he was not about to take sides against kin, so he arranged my imprisonment and then arranged for my escape. He gave me Pelar as a parting wage and threw in Macou, whom I had been training, as a bonus for my swift departure. I believe Lasmir Du liked me. A quick temper and a propensity for throwing people down wells are not considered flaws in Dree. As for Macou, I have never seen his like. From our first encounter when I fed him from my hand (a dangerous method I assure you) he has responded to me with quick intelligence. He seems almost to read my thoughts. His training was so swift as to scarcely justify the word.

"On one point alone did he resist me. He refused to take the hood, preferring to determine for himself his sight and sleeping. An odd point that. I sometimes imagine him to be a prince or sorcerer under an enchantment. But that is a crazy notion, fit only for dreams or fireside tales."

He paused a moment, lost in his reverie. "The cage which was lost in the storm . . ." he began, then stopped. Suddenly he remembered their situation. He remembered the gypsy's previous sullen silence. *Why did I have to mention the storm?* he thought. *And why did I call attention to it by faltering?*

Nara looked at him impassively. "Go on," she said, and in that moment something passed between the two of them. Britar knew that a bond had been forged by his act of forgetfulness and her forgiving of the hurt.

"The cage," he continued, giving Willan a sidelong glance to see if the magician understood what had just transpired, "was not for imprisonment. I had it made for Macou in Thile after seeing his agitation in crowds. The latching mechanism was simple and Macou himself could easily work it. He could come and go at will yet still feel a measure of protection from groping hands. Many people in this world do not know to leave an unusual animal alone. Many such fools reside in cities where all animals save common pets and vermin are unusual. So in a city, Macou prefers the cage to freedom. Of course he does not much care for cities, a feeling with which I sometimes concur." Britar grinned. "At least in the morning sunshine with a hangover, bruises, and empty pockets, I find cities not to my liking. Yet for some reason I usually leave a town at night." He looked at Willan in ironic innocence. "Why do you suppose that is?"

Willan snorted in mock disgust.

The hills which mark the northern border of R'thern end with some abruptness. After a gradual opening and thinning of the landscape, the traveler suddenly finds himself on the steep descent to the high plain country of northern R'thern.

On the Norther Plain, as in the hills, the rains come only in the winter months. During the summer the dominant color is brown, relieved only by the light green tracing of the occasional snow-fed stream. When the rains come, the streams swell and often overflow their banks. The riot of vegetation that results, tall grasses laced with flowers and puffballs, reaches far to the south, nearly to the city R'tha itself.

"Look to the east," said Willan to his companions as they descended from the hills. "Perhaps the day is clear enough to see the great aqueduct. It is a score of leagues from here, but at times the air is clear enough to allow it to be seen at such distances. Or so I have heard."

"It is within my sight," said Nara, "but I am unsure as to its visibility. I see with more than my eyes and I do sometimes confuse the abilities."

For his own part Britar could make out nothing for his strainings, save perhaps a slight darkening of the line that was the horizon.

"It may be only memory that places it so clearly before me," Willan admitted. "The aqueduct is a wondrous device. It was constructed more than a thousand years ago. No magic was used in its manufacture. It predates sorcery. I take comfort from such prodigies. Though wizards die and our skills atrophy, greatness may still be obtained through so mundane an act as putting stone to stone."

They descended swiftly. The great brown plain beneath them was only just beginning to awaken to the first hints of wetness that would revive it from parched summer slumber. For now, the air was still warm and dry. The stream beside them ran swiftly from the early rainfall in the hills. The narrow strip of green beside the stream had already begun its yearly outward creep of resurrection. But it would still be months before the water overflowed its banks.

"There!" called Willan, pointing. "A wild horse upon that hillside. This stream should lead us to some demesne where we may purchase a horse for Nara."

The Norther Plains abounded with ranches where cattle were raised and wild horses caught and brought to market. Before spring came, the land would be plainly marked with the crossings of the herds, and men would come to steal tribute from the prairie.

"I suggest that I should be the one to make the purchase," said Britar, "while both of you hold back. I have had some experience in horse trading. Moreover, my clothing is coarser than yours and that sometimes helps allay the suspicions of graziers and bucolics."

"Ye might be taken for a servant," said Nara.

"What of it?" said Britar. "The rich pay less than do the poor. That is how wealth is maintained."

"I only meant that ye might not wish to appear to be in servitude," she said. "Yer a Freelander, after all, and . . ."

"Fah!" said Britar. "Even in Dree I was my own man. Do you think that I care for appearances? If it would help our cause I would go in rags."

It took nearly two days for them to reach habitation, although signs of man became evident soon after they came to the foot of the hills and rode onto the plain. They passed a small watering hole, filled with water diverted from the stream, but stagnant and with an untended look. Nearby was a makeshift corral, in need of repair. After an hour's ride they encountered a ramshackle hut, meant for temporary use during the hectic time of spring. "Little happens during this time of year," Willan explained. "I have never been here in the fall. The land still sleeps in hot repose. In the spring the nomadic horsemen come, but now the plains are nearly deserted. Only the owners of the land remain."

They rode on. As the miles passed the travelers felt some creeping dismay at the signs of disuse which they encountered. Each of the three pondered, yet did not voice, the imminence of war and its demands upon men.

At length they came to the manor house, if so decrepit a building deserved the name. The boxlike structure had few windows, but many cracks showed between rough hewn boards that formed its walls. The wood of its construction had never seen paint or whitewash. The sun had bleached it to a solid gray. The entire scene gave the appearance of determined indolence. This place at least was no harbinger of war. It bespoke years of neglect.

Britar dismounted at a distance and slowly walked the dusty path that led to the house. There was an alcove set into the front of the building where the entry door would ordinarily be. Just inside, within the shaded inset porch, there stood a large stuffed chair. In that chair sat a wrinkled man who slowly fanned himself with a dull green fan.

"Are you the owner of this place?" asked Britar.

"I be that," said the man.

He was as weathered as his house, his features angular. His look was sharp, belying the languid manner of his movements. Beneath the coarse lines of his forehead, his eyes flickered like those of some greedy rodent. *I know that look*, thought Britar. *It speaks of dishonest weights and livestock watered just before sale*. Suppressing the desire to turn and walk away, Britar said, "My interest lies in horses. We require an additional mount, to ease my horse's burden and to give conveyance to the lady there."

The man looked sourly from Britar to the mounted pair who waited in the middle distance. "The 'lady' has the gypsy look to her," he said, his pebble-smooth voice betraying an undertone of roughness. "I do not like gypsies. She'll rob from you, mark it well. She'll steal your eyes."

Britar smiled a market smile, pushing aside the insult. "Not even a gypsy can ride without a horse," he said. "We require one."

The man spat upon the wooden floor. "In the back," he said. He got up and brushed past Britar into the sun. As he shuffled around toward the rear of the house his every motion indicated resentment at Britar's intrusion. Britar waved his friends to remain where they waited. Then he hurried after the man.

The horses were kept in a small pen that connected to a stable. Britar guessed that the wild roaming horses that they had seen were caught, broken and sent to market as fast as could be arranged, with little time and feed expended in the effort. *He probably does not even direct the enterprise himself*, Britar thought. *He hires it done by others*.

"There they be," the small gray man intoned. "Choose and I'll quote the price."

Britar made a point of walking around the pen to get a clear view of all the animals inside. Not counting a donkey, there were five mares and a gelding in the enclosure. But it was clear that only one of them was of any value as a mount. She was a sturdy creature, sorrel-colored with gray speckles dusting her side. The other five beasts were either aging or decrepit. Britar dismissed them without a second thought.

"I would like to see the roan," he said. The owner nodded and entered the corral. Britar also entered but the man motioned for him to remain by the fence. The owner entered the stable and brought forth a simple bridle which he put on the mare. He led the animal to the side of the pen where Britar waited.

"A good horse," he said while Britar made the customary examination of tooth, leg, and hoof. "You'll not find better within several days' ride."

"The price?" asked Britar.

"Six gold muners," the man replied.

Britar scowled. "Surely three would be a fairer price."

"For the impoverished," the man replied, "I will sell yon gray dapple for but a single muner." He indicated a horse so swaybacked that she resembled a cooked sausage.

Britar stroked the flank of the horse before him. No flesh sagged here. He backed away, lost his footing slightly and stumbled into the man behind him. "Your pardon," Britar said. "I have lost the way of pasture walking. I am no longer good at avoiding things underfoot." He smiled sheepishly. "Four gold muners for the roan," he said.

The man shook his head and held up his hand. First five fingers were displayed, then one. "Six," he said. "I include the bridle."

"Worth a copper talen, perhaps," said Britar.

The man shrugged. "There are no other mounts within a day's ride. Few other demesnes deal in horses at this time of year. Let the gypsy ride a donkey; it is all the same to me. But make your decision. I dislike visitors."

Britar reached into his pouch and produced six coins of yellow gold.

They rode from the ranch toward the south. Clouds blew before the sun and away again.

"This is a fine mount," said Nara. "How much did you pay?"

"Six gold muners," admitted Britar.

"Six!" exclaimed Willan in surprise. "Exorbitant. Did you

not say that you had skill in the trading of horses?"

"Such skill is useless against perversity," muttered Britar. "The man was sour, shriveled, and would have sent us away with nothing. Skills other than trading were required."

The other two looked at him in puzzlement. "Skills?" Nara asked.

Britar smiled. "While we haggled, I contrived to remove four gold muners from his purse. The man is a fool; he keeps his money about his person even when at home. Such distrust should be rewarded from time to time. . . ."

Chapter Ten

The autumn night was clear. Macou had preyed a goose at dusk, swooping down upon a migratory stray to tear her from the sky. Pine needles crackled in the campfire, giving off a pungent scent and flavoring the goose that roasted above the flames. It made a welcome contrast to the standard travel fare of coarse black bread and salted meat.

The trio praised the falcon's exploits between steaming mouthfuls. Britar fed his pet by hand, presenting choice morsels of food to him and stroking his feathered head. The thief smiled. "Ah, I'd almost forgotten what contentment felt like," he said with a sigh, stretching his powerful arms above his head lazily. "And though I despair to break this mood, still, a question nags me. Has anyone considered what we will *do* once we reach R'tha?"

Willan looked at Britar in pensive silence. Then he said, "I have given the matter some thought. What we need most is simple information—information concerning Quecora and his acts. But how do we learn of him and yet escape his notice? And how do we hinder him in his awful tasks and yet retain our lives?"

Nara twisted slightly where she sat crosslegged on the ground and rested her head upon her hands, her dark hair shielding her eyes. "For myself," she said, "I am hampered by a single line of Sight. My vision is clear, but the monster looms too large for me to see the whole of him. The ground around him is dangerous besides. I must work through other eyes, see through other perspectives. That way I will build up a picture of the many parts that make up the whole."

"How can we arrange this for you?" Willan asked.

"I require physical contact with those whose eyes I will use," she replied carefully. "I must meet with the actors in the play, speak with them, touch them. As friend Britar pilfers from pockets, so must I pilfer from souls."

"Is this not dangerous?" Britar asked.

"Yes," she said. "Some aspects more than others. Much information can be gained at little risk by simple fortune-telling tricks. The questions asked are often more revealing than the answers they require. As for the touching . . ." She shrugged. "The closer to the Beast, the more danger. I would prefer to work a trysting if such a thing can be arranged."

"A trysting?" Willan echoed. "To call up the spirits of the dead?"

She smiled. "That is one of the functions of a trysting. There is some debate as to the origin of the entities invoked. A trysting of many people creates a quickening of the collective will. Memories become animate. Imagination gains substance. Some skeptical practitioners have maintained that tryst ghosts seldom yield information that could not have been obtained by a careful examination of the memories of the trysting group. Others disagree. However, a trysting sees through many eyes, yet presents no single aspect to the suspicious foe. If one moves swiftly, with determination and subterfuge, it might be possible to steal knowledge from even Quecora himself. We might map the Demon's plans; I could place him within the landscape of my art without his full knowledge of the deed." She smiled a smile that substituted cold irony for mirth. "If not, if our enemy takes suspicion, who knows? Perhaps some innocent will deflect the blow. The sleigh sometimes escapes by throwing the weak and helpless to the wolves."

Britar felt a chill at this remark. It reminded him that there was still much that was hidden about this woman and her dark possibilities. Willan, however, seemed not to notice Britar's unease.

"A trysting of the principals, eh?" the wizard mused. "Carnival time in R'tha approaches. Carnival marks the end of mourning, the birth of revelry. The new King forms a new court. Perhaps . . . many things are possible at Carnival." He stared for a moment into space. "I must think on this," he said. The silence stretched for a time and then Willan looked at Britar as if to bring forth the large man's thoughts.

Britar roused himself from his brooding. There was no need to voice a transitory unease. He drew a breath and said, "I know little of R'tha. I have not been there. I cannot help plan the assault. My city skills you know by now. Gambling, theft and brawling. I am not skilled at drinking though I have had some practice of and inclination toward the art. I suspect that I will be useless at intrigue. If you conceive a task, inform me; I will help as I can."

Willan nodded. "Very well," he said. "I have much to ponder as we travel. Rest now. We must reach the city before Carnival begins."

During the next day's ride, Britar's thoughts were never far from the dark witch who rode beside him. Who was this Nara? he wondered. What did they know of her true nature? He searched his memory for some recollection of the Yani, her people, but the attempt was fruitless. Gypsies were rarities in Freeland; witches were rarer still.

Drawing close to Nara, he said, "The man from whom I purchased your horse is no friend of the gypsies. He implied that you are a jade; he said outright that you are likely a thief! I do not understand. What have the gypsies done to engender such sentiment?"

Nara shrugged, the subject being too worn to give rise to emotion. "Hatred is a sturdy weed. It grows everywhere. My people are seldom on good terms with outsiders. Constant movement weakens the ties of etiquette and conscience.

"Where I was born there is a mountain, honeycombed with caves. It is used as a meeting place by my people. We come, we go; the visits are short, but there is always a population within the mountain. The valley below is lush and for a time enjoyed a fashion as a summer place for nobility. Some of the Yani have conducted 'tours' through the mountain in order that young princes might satisfy their curiosity. Invariably, at some point in the expedition the lights fail and money vanishes. When the lights are rekindled, oh, much apology! How could such a thing occur? And under our protection? Oh shame and tragedy!" She brought her hand to her forehead in mock anguish. "But no restitution is made," she continued sarcastically. "No miscreants are produced. No one is punished. The young nobles leave, their curiosity blunted if not assuaged. Certainly their gullibility has been pruned along with their purses."

She gave Britar a sidelong glance. "Do ye know anything of the history of the gypsies? Our skin marks us as having bred in sunny climes, yet we are now found only in the north. I myself was born in Pasa Del, a land of cold fogs and snow. Early in the years of the Demon, before even the wars began, Quecora discovered that the Yani could not be controlled or deceived. Others fell to enthrallment and lies, but my people had too much of the Sight to accept bribery or the promise of power. We saw the blackness of his blandishments; we knew the emptiness of the future he offered. Even the worst among us knew the taint that surrounded Quecora like a shroud. We called him Beast, and we fled his touch.

"Our knowledge doomed us. Quecora decreed our extermination. His armies demanded our heads as part tribute. From any given town, his legions demanded corn, wheat, beef, gold, and the heads of gypsies. Whole villages were put to the torch for offering us sanctuary. We were gathered up like cattle and fed to fiery pits or cut to ribbons as food for dogs.

"Pasa Del at that time was ruled by Tongué, the first of Quecora's allies. Tongué was a human devil who rose to power by assassination and wholesale slaughter. His armies invented the practice of ringing a town with pyres of burning brimstone and antimony, choking the inhabitants' lives away. His spies had a standing order to remove the tongues of those who said a word against his rule. He had these trophies displayed at his palace. The tongues of Tongué he called them in jest.

"And yet here is a fact most strange: the gypsies in Pasa Del

were safe from the atrocities of the Beast. Of all my people,
the only ones who did not die were in the country of Tongué
the madman, Tongué the tyrant. He was too valued an ally to
be pressed even by Quecora on this one issue. So the Yani in
this one place lived, saved by a murderer, when better men
offered us up to the abattoir. The ironies of history are as
great as its lessons are grim. The Yani seldom believe in good
fortune or the kindness of the gods. Still less do we believe in
the kindness of men. There is for us only the toss of the
coins."

Britar felt cold.

The high plains become the low plains and the low plains
are bisected by the Jo. The Jo is a brackish trickle of a river in
the summer, a swirling torrent by winter's light. To the travelers crossing it in autumn it was a shallow stream that barely
wet the pasterns of their mounts.

They traveled without incident. Shortly, only the Malant
Hills lay between them and R'tha. A swift climb, passage
along a ridge and the hills were nearly done. Soon they would
sight the city where it lay between the hills and the river Yes.

It was nearly dark, yet Willan urged his companions to
greater speed. He wanted to camp within sight of the city. Britar shrugged at this. He had never seen R'tha and would have
been content to postpone the event until morning; however,
he complied with Willan's urging.

As darkness gathered, Britar began to wonder if they were
to attempt progress even into the night. His companions
could see in the dark, he knew; but neither he nor the horses
possessed that faculty. He was about to voice complaint
when they crested a hill and darkness vanished.

R'tha glowed. The stones of its construction had that prop-
erty. Heat rising from the cooling plain made the city sparkle
like a cluster of stars that had drifted to the earth. In one district the predominant hue was topaz, in another,
aquamarine. Toward the center of the city, spires and pillars
rose to terminate in teardrop bulbs and geometric domes.
Public parks were dotted by small ceremonial pyramids that
shifted color according to the rites therein. The larger temples

cast a glow that merged with the light of the newly risen moon as it edged upward from the horizon. In the older portions of the city, the light was mottled, for damage and uneven weathering will alter glowstones' texture. Some call the uneven radiation unhealthy; some say that it invigorates. Squalor is like that: exciting and debilitating. Old buildings become tenements and the streets between them teem with life and death.

High towers grew from the city's heart, while squat buildings lurked about its edges like a massive ring of mushrooms. One aspect only violated the pattern: near the edges of R'tha, five green towers rose in perfect symmetry like emerald flames.

"Jahf's Towers," murmured Willan, as they dismounted.

"Eh?" said Britar.

"The five green towers," said Willan. "Had you not heard of them? They were built by the great Jahf, who designed the present city with sorcery and geometry. Once they stood at the very edge of the city. R'tha grew past them, then was pruned back by the clashes of the Demon War. Now it has grown again.

"The towers are a defense, you see, or rather, they were a defense until the lore was lost. They stand at the corners of a pentacle." Willan removed D'tias and traced a glowing figure on the ground.

"A pentacle inscribed within a pentagon does itself contain a smaller pentagon. The series five times repeats itself, and there, at the points of the fifth star, stand the turrets of the Palace of the King's Light." Willan paused for a moment, pensive and ironic. "The Palace light has dimmed somewhat. Once it could outshine the sun. Five adepts would place themselves within the towers of the palace and apply their skills. The Fingers would resonate, as the body of a lute resonates to the plucking of a string or the striking of a chord. With this resonance the city becomes divorced from the bonds which tie it firmly to the earth. It no longer quite partakes of worldly time. Nothing may enter or leave, save air and ether and even those substances may cross the barrier in trickles only.

"During the War the city of R'tha was besieged. The Demon's main force, a horrible collection of mercenaries, thralls and things which could not die, thought to topple the city in a matter of days. Instead, the shield of R'tha held that savage legion at bay for nearly a season! Meanwhile, Quecora's army exhausted the resources of the countryside and then began to starve while the great General Buri collected a makeshift force of peasant warriors from the outlying districts. It was Quecora's first great defeat, some say the turning point of the War. Quecora abandoned R'thern to turn his attention to the Southern Continent and to the wars at sea."

Willan's voice became quiet, nearly a whisper. "There were originally twenty wizards with the duty of the Towers. At the end of the siege, there were left but four. The rest had lost their arts or their lives to exhaustion."

Nara broke her silence. "I thought that the Towers required one adept in each. Five sorcerers would seem to be the minimum for the spell."

"That is true," Willan said. "It is also true that in the final hours of the siege, with Buri's force approaching, when Quecora made his last desperate attempts to breach the Towers' radiance, there were but four magicians still in possession of their faculties. And it is a fact that the defenses held. I do not know the answer to the paradox. Perhaps the rule of Five is not unbreakable. Or perhaps one of the Four learned the secret of being in two places simultaneously."

Britar asked, "Did no one question the magicians after the battle?"

Willan smiled coldly. "A fruitless task. All were quite mad. The first was found apparently paralyzed, muscles locked in what one presumes was some ritual posture. The second was asleep and never awoke. The third was talkative enough, even to empty air, but the language that he spoke has never been deciphered. The fourth merely refused all human intercourse and spent the remainder of his days in solitude, playing pentatonic melodies on a small silver harp."

Chapter Eleven

Before the coming of the Demon, three great cities grew upon the Northern Continent: Thile, Praxis, and R'tha. After the holocaust only R'tha remained. Thile was overrun, destroyed; only the ruins of elder Thile still remain, upriver from the new city that now bears that name. Of Praxis there remains no trace. Dim legends only speak of a city to the south, a city of wondrous beauty and accomplishment. A city that was, and now is not.

They entered R'tha at first light, when the river mist still crouched upon the streets, diademing flagstones with jewels of aqueous light. The city stirred about them, poised halfway between slumber and awakening.

Street vendors rattled their wares as they took up their stations along the broad thoroughfare that led into the city from the north. Through the center of the street clopped a horse pulling a wagon filled with ice. The precious cargo had come by barge from the glaciers at the headwaters of the Yes. From within a shabby building a baby cried. A cockcrow echoed overhead.

To one side there was a scurry and a flurry and a pile of garbage erupted with motion. Several rats spewed forth, pursued by a cat intent upon a lively breakfast. Seeing the activity, several feline onlookers howled encouragement; one leaped from behind a door to join the chase.

As the trio rode past, another cat upon a windowsill ceased

its howling, struck dumb with the sight of Macou perched on Britar's shoulder. Here perhaps is some sport, the cat might have thought at first, but soon the carnivorous intent withered before the intensity of the falcon's gaze, and the cat, feigning disinterest, dropped its stare and retreated through the open window.

"How much farther to the Palace?" asked Britar.

"Patience," said Willan. "The city is large, and we still have far to go. We have not yet reached the elder city wall."

The city's origins were lost in the myths of antiquity. One legend held that the Forest of Beginning once grew in the fields that lay across the marshes from the city's present site. In the center of the forest grew a tree that bore animate fruit. First this Tree of Life grew fishes, which fell into the marshes and from there found their way to populate the seas. Insects followed, then a year of toads and frogs. Reptiles replaced these, then birds, then verminous mammals and finally manlike creatures, the ancestors of humanity. These precursors to humankind felled the forest, including the Tree of Life.

Whatever the city's origins, later events are well recorded. Two millennia previous, the city rose to primitive grandeur, fell and rose again. The great aqueduct was constructed before the fifty years' drought, on advice of Wandel the Prophet, whose name is still a blessing and a curse upon the lips of the workers of the fields. The Age of Sorcery followed, sputtering to life first upon the continent of the Toltans, then taking flame throughout the world. Noble Jahf, first of the sorcerer kings, rebuilt R'tha almost in its entirety. Only scattered random enclaves of older buildings remained, these being distinguished by their granite construction, which neither shines nor seems to decay.

The morning grew to full activity as the travelers approached the city's inner gates. The walls of the city proper stood much lower than is usual for defense. The Five Towers were meant to be the main obstruction to attack; the walls had been added almost as an afterthought. They had been strengthened after the Demon War, and the failure of the sorcery necessary to the Five.

Today the gates of the city were flung wide for the day before the first night of Carnival. Gleaming metal strands festooned the walls; incense burners filled the air with myriad smells: juniper, apple, gentian and pine. Hawkers' cries were likewise ubiquitous, proffering a thousand and one small items at high markup: scarves, candies, jewelry, religious icons.

The crowds had a restive air, as well they might. Before Carnival comes *Whar,* a time of general mourning and repentance. The more ascetic religions use *Whar* as a time of fasting, silence, or solitude and meditation. Taxes are paid at the beginning of *Whar* and it had become a custom for debts to be repaid or forgiven during this period also. The exact length of the holidays is astrologically determined, *Whar* usually being about three weeks and Carnival ten days.

A King who dies during the summer or fall is embalmed and held in state until the fifth day of *Whar* when he is buried. His heir becomes King in a somber ceremony at dawn the next day and spends the remainder of the time of *Whar* in seclusion. Carnival then celebrates his ascension to the throne and a new court begins. The twin holidays of *Jaicon* and *Jaicona* at the end of spring serve the same function should the King die in winter or spring. Only sudden war or similar disasters may hurry the process of succession.

The trio left their horses in the public stables just inside the gates of R'tha. After some discussion and inquiry, Britar located a facility to which he was willing to entrust Macou. Willan grew impatient with the dickering and wasted time, but there was no help for it. Macou was too obvious an accouterment and their plan required a certain stealth. As they walked toward the center of the city, Willan explained his intent.

"A principal segment of the population of the Palace is devoted to providing entertainment. In fact, performers are outnumbered only by menials and equeries. Not only must the Court itself be kept amused, but also the populace of R'tha has grown accustomed to the divertissements provided in the public theaters adjacent to the Palace. Commonly, new entertainers are auditioned after a long procedure involving petition, recommendation, and so forth. But there is today a new King, with new tastes, dissimilar to the old. So public auditions will be held." Willan pointed to a notice upon the wall. It bore the inscribed pentagram symbol of the royal family. "You see? New entertainers are to appear at the World Pavilion, annex to the north Palace wall.

"This is Carnival. Jaded tastes crave novelty. We may gain entry to the Palace, even presence at the great Carnival feasts by merely . . . Eh? What is it?"

The trio's path had taken them away from the crowds. A corner's turn and they walked alongside a great stone wall, obviously of ancient construction. With the sight of the bulwark, Nara's step had suddenly faltered, and she clutched at both her staff and Britar's arm for support.

"What is the matter?" asked Britar as he placed an arm around her waist to steady her.

"I . . . I . . ." She swallowed as if to clear a lump from her throat. She took a deep, ragged breath and straightened her back. Another breath.

"I am not accustomed to such . . . antiquity," she said in a whispery voice. She shook her head as if to drive from it an unwanted sight. "The past of these stones is like a chasm, filled with mist. I see—flashes. The history attempts to overwhelm the present." She closed her eyes tightly, then opened them again. The gold of her eyes slowly cleared. She smiled weakly. "I had anticipated only a little of this. No, that is untrue. I did not expect this at all. I did not know that I possessed a fear of such heights." She looked at Willan. "Ye must realize that while this is level ground, to Time we are surrounded by ragged, mountainous territory. New and transient structures coexist with the aged and ageless. I've learned through past experience to block out the overwhelming histories of crowds. The memories of humankind are complex, but shallow. These stones remember ages. This new phenomenon is . . . well, it is new to me. I've not been in a city since my coming to the Sight."

"Can you walk?" asked Willan. "Will you be able to . . ."

"I am all right," she interrupted. "This caught me by surprise, that is all. I'll not hinder our task." With that she shook off Britar's support and strode purposefully down the path before them. The two men hurried to overtake her.

Though their path carried them through the less traveled back streets, still they encountered crowds anticipating Carnival. At one street corner a fanatic hectored an unheeding mass of passersby, reminding them of their sins and weaknesses. Street musicians played at various sites. On one street no less than four such entertainers could be heard simultaneously, to disconcerting effect, since they played on disharmonious scales and used greatly dissimilar instruments.

As the trio approached the center of the city, the urban pattern became more regular. The overall pentagonal geometry merged with a spiraling network of streets that all led to the complex of monarchical buildings surrounding the Palace of Light.

From a smiling vendor, they purchased a meal of sweet bread and light wine, which they devoured while they walked. They were just completing the last few bites and swallows when they reached the great public square at the north face of the Palace. Directly in front of them stood the World Pavilion.

The Pavilion was a large open structure adjacent to the Palace and connected to it by an arching bridge which leapt from the Pavilion roof to an exterior battlement of the Palace walls. The Pavilion sides could be closed off by curtains or the building could be divided by this means into numerous smaller areas.

The square was not crowded; most of those present were in or near the Pavilion, availing themselves of an afternoon's free entertainment. After nightfall, however, the Carnival festivities would begin, and the area would boil with noise and merriment.

The trio made their way through the crowd which milled about the entrance of the Pavilion. For the auditions, a small stage had been erected in the center of the enclosure. Off to one side sat a man of authority, to judge from his dress, demeanor, and the manner in which the performers addressed their actions in his direction (though not too obviously, for such would be a gross breach of etiquette and proper showmanship). Clearly, this man was the Judge of the proceedings; his opinion would determine which of the performers would receive an invitation to the Palace, which would be subsidized as part of the general Carnival activities, and which would be sent away.

Upon the stage a dwarf was attempting to sing a ballad of unrequited love. The crowd was not appreciative. Scattered coughs and catcalls interrupted the song. Willan and his companions made their way to a registration line at the rear of the Pavilion. While they waited, the singer finished, and was replaced by an inept escape artist. The bonds with which the unfortunate man contested had been expertly tied by one of the King's Guard. The restraints also included several metal shackles with locks. After several minutes of futile struggle, the poor man was lifted bodily from the stage, amid peals of laughter from the crowd. A musician took the stage and began to play intricate tunes in a minor mode upon a wooden flute. At length the three reached the front of the line where waited a functionary with a stylus and a waxboard tablet.

"Your name, please?" the man said in a not unfriendly voice.

"Willan of B'ru," Willan replied, "and Nara of Pasa Del, and . . . a servant."

"Where is B'ru?" the man inquired.

"It is the name of my clan," said Willan. "I am from the southern hills, though I have resided in R'tha for several years."

"I see," the man said. He indicated Nara with his glance. "Are the two of you a single act?"

"No," said Willan. "We perform separately, but we make application to the Court as a single entity."

"Unusual, unusual," the man murmured. "What is your skill?"

"I am a thaumaturge," said Willan.

The man nodded, scribbled something, turned to Nara and said smoothly, "You are Yani, I perceive. We see few gypsies in R'tha, to our sorrow. Are you a fortune teller?"

"I am a Seer," Nara replied with a slight trace of hauteur in her voice. "Those of talent such as mine seldom perform in public. We find the process wearisome. The King's Court would be an exception, of course, but I'd rather dispense with this formality," she indicated the stage with a sweep of her hand. "If such a thing may be allowed. Here, a demonstration." She touched the man's arm lightly, then looked him in the face.

"Yer name is Weltan; ye are married with three children. Yer mother still lives with you. Ye had a fight with your wife three days ago. After the fight ye went to see your mistress Leoneta, who lives across the river. Yer wife does not know of Leoneta, though she suspects, which is why the two of ye did fight. Ye bought yer wife flowers the next day. Ye bought Leoneta a wrought iron ring. Shall I tell ye what the iron does signify?"

Weltan blanched slightly, coughed and licked his lips. "Ah . . . Yes . . . I mean, no! Uh, very impressive," he murmured. He drew in his breath and managed to suppress a nervous giggle. He looked anxiously at Willan. "You have no objection to the audition, I hope?" Willan shook his head. "Ah . . ." Weltan began again. "Good. Fine. I am sure that I can convince the Lord to allow you to stand for all three. I will note that the ability of the . . . the Lady here is safely vouched." He pointed to seats in front of the crowd near the stage. "Please wait up front until it is time for you to perform." Weltan turned from them and motioned to the next hopeful in the line to advance.

As they walked up an aisle to the waiting area in front of the stage, Britar caught Nara's eye and grinned. Her smile of reply was thin-lipped, but it bespoke of mischief satisfied.

The waiting seemed to stretch interminably, the acts before them providing little in the way of diversion for their impatience. The sun's light began to slant beneath the building's roof. Britar began to consider categories for the acts. The *Excellent* category was barely populated. More numerous were the singers who could scarcely sing, thumb-fingered musicians, disobedient animals, lame jesters, and dwarf acrobats. There seemed to be an unusual number of acts in the last category. *We come late in this process*, thought Britar. *The cream has been already skimmed; the milk begins to curdle.*

Finally, it was Willan's turn to take the stage. Donning a black cape, he stepped forward.

As Willan mounted the small raised platform, his manner changed. Previously, he had seemed plain, withdrawn. One would not notice him on the street. But now a vibrancy entered his expression, his movements became fluid and vivid. He swept the room with his gaze and he smiled.

Willan held up his left hand, the palm facing away from the audience. With his right forefinger he pointed to the back of his left hand and raised an eyebrow. He clenched a fist, then opened it again. A blue ball appeared between the first two fingers of his left hand. He repeated the movement. The ball was changed to green. Again. Two balls appeared, both blue.

In bewildering succession the spheres multiplied and were transformed. Now two, now three, red, blue, green, and yellow, they seemed to dart from thumb to finger like magpies perching upon a tree. Suddenly there appeared an orange cube. Willan looked at it for a moment, plucked it from his left hand with his right, shrugged, then tossed it over his shoulder. It vanished in a puff of smoke. His left hand continued sprouting balls.

Willan stopped the display, three balls nestled between four fingers. He looked out at the audience which had by now begun to follow his actions with some interest. He tossed the balls into the air and commenced to juggle. He laughed. His voice contained a resonance that carried to the back of the arena.

"I learned my few poor thaumaturgical skills at the feet of my father, who was wiser and far more skilled than I. He told me once, 'Entertainment is the goal, and to reach that goal you must capture and hold the attention of your audience. You must deal in universals, subjects of interest to everyone, such as life, death, and money.' "

Willan smiled. "The creation of life requires far more time than is available to me. Death is swift, but I am a coward, and no good at taking risks. That leaves money."

Suddenly, with a twist of his hands, two of the juggled spheres became bright coins which sparkled in the air. So sudden yet graceful was the mutation that several of the onlookers gasped.

"I fear," said Willan, "that while my father gave me much advice he gave me little money. The trick requires another coin. Sire?" said Willan looking at the Judge. "Would you lend me but a single coin for the duration of my time? I will return it."

The Judge grunted and produced a small coin from his purse. A servant boy took it to Willan who accepted it, placed it in the juggling stream and banished the final ball to limbo, all in the blink of an eye.

"Ah," said Willan. "That is better. Money prefers its own kind." He laughed again. "Money!" he exclaimed and looked out over the crowd. "Do I now have your attention? I thought as much. Money always commands respect, does it not? We need money and we love money, do we not? It can buy so many things. For instance food!" He stamped his foot and one of the coins was replaced by an egg, soaring in the air from hand to hand.

Two coins and an egg now bobbled back and forth. Willan continued, "And next to food, what is important? Shelter perhaps? Protection from the elements? Wood for the fire? How about fire itself?" He stamped his foot again and one of the coins caught fire. In the audience Britar scowled. There had been no flash from Willan's ring. Was this then merely a trick?

"Ouch," said Willan in comical display. "Juggling fire is a painful task and my time is nearly up. Yet I could not leave without a bow to love and beauty. What are food and shelter without the finer things, eh? So thus!" He stamped and the final coin was replaced by a red flower which filled the air with fragrance.

"My time is up, I think," said Willan. "Yet let me make one last observation. The wise man does not squander his money. He husbands it and makes it grow. He sends it out to do his bidding and if he watches it well, then it returns to him. La!"

Willan tossed the egg high into the air, then with a single motion threw the flower to a young girl and hurled the flaming ember out over the crowd. The ember puffed and only smoke remained. Willan clapped both hands to the falling egg. There was a crunch of breaking eggshell and a woman squealed. When Willan opened his hands three coins rested in his palms.

There was scattered applause and Willan vaulted from the stage. "Thank you, Sire," said Willan, pressing the coin into the Judge's hand. "I am most grateful." The Judge grunted and placed the coin into his purse. Willan gestured to his companions and the trio left the hall.

"I suggest that we go separate ways for the evening," Willan told his companions. "I have business to attend to in preparation for tomorrow's entry to the Palace and tomorrow evening's entertainment. Besides, we draw less note as individuals. I propose that we reconvene at this spot tomorrow noon."

"That seems reasonable," said Britar. "The notion of Carnival begins to be appealing. A night of it sits well with me. But what if, despite the admitted excellence of your performance, the Judge does not decide in favor of our appointment to the Court?"

Willan smiled. "He will appoint us. The Judge is an intelligent and subtle man. He approves of these qualities in others." Britar looked blank. "The coin which he gave me for use in my performance was copper," Willan explained. "The coin that I returned to him was gold."

"I see," said Britar, for he did indeed.

Chapter Twelve

Nara the gypsy walked through the streets of R'tha with slow and wary stride. She was afraid.

Despite her forceful words to Willan and Britar, she did not know if she could fully control the flood of sensation which the Sight of the city could provoke within her. Anything less than total control might prove disastrous to their mission; yet she had managed to terminate the incident at the stone wall only by fully suppressing her clairvoyance. Her reading of poor Weltan had required an eyeblink only. Such tactics would be of little use in seeking knowledge of the Demon. Subtlety and grace of the highest art would be required to tap so dangerous a wellspring. But the experience of temporal vertigo had left her feeling clumsy and awkward. Her grip tightened about her staff and she drew upon the channels of strength that it contained. Could she expand her skill so swiftly? Could she inure herself to the Sight of chasmed centuries of time? In but a few short hours? She drank her staff's strength again. She could; she would. She must.

Very well then, she thought. It is time to begin. Her course angled over to a building's site. She stood upright with her back against the cool stone facade. She wrapped her thoughts around her breath and listened to her pulse. Time slowed to a crawl.

There were only a few pedestrians upon this particular walkway. Most were self-engrossed and barely saw the gypsy, striking though she was. The few who noticed assumed that she was a reveler or a courtesan awaiting an assignation. Their unguarded souls were easy to examine.

She let her vision expand and the scene grew in dimension and complexity. Each passerby became a thread in a woven tapestry of memory and context. Each carried with them scenes of past importance. Some wore their origins like an honored cloak. Others carried a badge of shame and guilt. Upon some, life pressed down like a huge stone.

After a time the buildings round her began to whisper of their former times. This particular scene had little to divulge. She sensed a small parade in the not too distant past. Last holiday perhaps. Beyond that, nothing. It was a minor side street of little importance. It had few tales to tell. Good. She had entered the waters of the city's past as into a calm shallow pool. She cocked her head and listened for the call of histories. Distant clamor came to her. She smiled. Her expression set, she once more began to walk. Into the past. To confront the tumbled tumult of what had been.

Britar of Freeland also roamed the streets of the city, his path aimless. After the nadir of activity during the heat of afternoon, the tempo of the day began to wax. The people bustled as the dusk descended. Britar drank deeply of the growing excitement. I could grow to love this city, he thought.

He bought a cooked fowl's leg from a vendor and munched upon it as he walked. His professional's eye noted easy pickings in the pockets and purses of the jostling throng, but he restrained himself. Even a slight risk was too much. How curious not to require more money than one had. But his funds were ample for the night; and tomorrow—tomorrow was a different world.

He moved by instinct, and his instincts led him toward the waterfront. One step back from the warehouses and docks was the nether region of bars and carnal houses and theaters for the vulgar tastes of the shoreman laborers. At every step down from the public opulence of the Palace toward the private squalor of coarse entertainments, Britar's mood lightened. Finally he spied a bar which even at dusk gave out music and laughter and the smell of smoke. He grinned. *There stands my place*, he thought.

He entered to the tune of a psaltery, played by a crone in the corner. The old woman plucked at the strings of the instrument with clawlike hands that moved in dancing spasms. Two barge workers, already drunk, tried to follow the simple tune with voices that substituted loudness for harmony.

The bar was horseshoe-shaped, extending to the middle of the room. To one side were games of cards and tossed coins and dice. Around the horseshoe bend in the opposite corner a dwarf was muttering darkly into a tankard of light ale.

"Cashiered . . ." the diminutive one was saying. "Pensioned off! After all these years! Old King Seilung liked the small folk. Not the new one, though. His head's lifted too high to even see us. He likes singers and conjurers. What's his name? The dumb prince who's King now? Tilviss? Tilwesser? Ha! Three score entertainers Seilung employed. Of the small folk, I mean." He turned to the nearest table full of people and extended a finger as if to emphasize a point. "And that's not counting a dozen or so midget serving girls. Think of it! Eighty, ninety or so of the little folk, out in the streets, barely enough money to live on, living off our wits. Ha! Our skills! You think we're useless! You think we don't have any talents? Look at this!"

The dwarf did a quick cartwheel to his left which brought him next to the startled Britar. "How's that!" the small acrobat exclaimed. "Even a few pints heavy I'm still centered and spry!"

The man behind the bar glowered at the dwarf for a moment, then said, "Hear me, Murley. I like you and your money is plenty good. But I cannot have you disturbing the other customers. I will buy you an ale if you promise not to do any more jumping about."

Murley made a face and said, "Ah, I meant no disturbance, Bori. I just . . ." His voice trailed off.

Britar held up two fingers, between which were copper coins. "Barman, if you will draw two tankards of ale for the pair of us, this good fellow and I will commandeer yon table." He indicated a corner table with his thumb. As the bar-

man moved to comply, Britar grinned at Murley. "My name is
Britar and it is my intention to get so drunk that all *my* dexterity will be required to lift the cup from table to mouth."

Murley grinned back, immediately warming to the heavy
man in front of him. "It's Carnival," he said. "To follow any
other plan is a serious breech of custom. I've violated manners once tonight; let's hope that it does not happen again." A
sly smile crept over his face. "At least until, oh, midnight,
shall we say?"

Britar grabbed his drink and thrust the other into Murley's
hands. "Is it possible to violate manners after midnight during Carnival?"

"Probably not," said Murley as they walked over to the table. "But the impossibility of the task should not keep any
man from the attempt."

Willan took a path similar in direction to that of his two allies: he set forth eastward, toward the river and away from
the setting sun. Unlike his friends, however, his course was
rapid and direct. He knew his destination. For several years,
he had called it home.

The capital of R'thern had two parts, separated by the Yes,
a wide river, very shallow at this point. The lesser of the two
parts of R'tha was given over to industry. Long low buildings,
open pavilions, small shops, and factories rose from what
had been marshland. The wet persisted, imperfectly drained,
and gave rise to clinging fogs. These fogs thickened with the
smoke of furnaces and smelter fumes. At night, the flare of
light from poured metals often illuminated the fog from beneath, giving the coiling vapors an eerie underglow. The
sparks of pounded ingots added to the spectacle. Gazing into
the shimmering, sparkling mists from a distance one could
well imagine the creation of galaxies, the manufacture of neb-
ulae, instead of the prosaic locks, buckles, ornaments and
handles which were in fact the products of the enterprise.

Willan bypassed the docks of the waterfront and crossed
one of the floating bridges that connected the southern portion of the city to the factories across the river and to the
fields beyond the wetlands. Upriver, the bridges were more

permanent constructions, arching over the water to allow the passage of barges underneath. Few barges went further south than R'tha. There was little beyond R'tha but desert.

Most of the traffic on the bridge was in the direction opposite to Willan's path. The foundry workers, apprentices, and farmers of the distant fields streamed westward, squinting at the sunset glare. They ignored Willan, their thoughts directed toward the delights of Carnival.

Willan soon attained the opposite shore and began to thread his way through the maze of squat stone buildings that began at the bridge's other end. His emotions were those of both familiarity and estrangement. It had taken years for the district to enter into his soul. It had taken only the past few months to divorce him from it once again. Eventually he arrived at his destination: a stone building of medium size, a thin wisp of smoke coiling from its roof to join the marshmist that grew in the dusk. Habit snatched at him and he checked the box beside the entranceway for any messages meant for him. The box was empty and he smiled. He rapped his fist against the overhead beam; the door stood half ajar.

"Ho, Mulau!" he called. "Are you still working so close to Carnival? What will the neighbors make of that?"

There were two persons inside, a slender man of late middle age and a young boy. The boy had been playing hand games with string in obvious boredom. The man was polishing a small brass figurine with a piece of emory cloth. At Willan's knock, he looked up, dropped the cloth and exclaimed, "Willan! You've returned!"

Mulau rushed across the workshop and the two men embraced. "Willan, Willan, my boy," repeated the older man. "Have you returned to stay? Will you . . . How long . . . I mean, ah hell, it's good to see you." He clapped the taller man on the back and hugged him again.

"A moment, Mulau," said Willan, turning to the boy, Mulau's apprentice, who had come to work there only a few months before Willan's departure. "Jon," Willan said. "Does Naco still have a stock of those clever bird cages of his?"

"I think so, sir," replied Jon politely.

"Well, then," said Willan, "run over to his shop and see if

he is still there. If he is, tell him that I want the biggest one he
has and that I will trade for it that chess set of mine that he so
admires." Willan winked at Jon. "If you are quick about it, I
will give you a silver piece with which to purchase Carnival
treats."

"Yes sir!" Jon exclaimed and vanished.

Mulau sighed. "You will not be staying long."

"I have always been an open book to you, Mulau," said
Willan.

"Fah!" replied the other man. "You are close-mouthed, se-
cretive and opaque, but I love you anyway. And I do know
you well enough to discern the obvious. This is not a home-
coming nor is it a social call."

Willan nodded. "Please do not be disappointed."

"Ah, disappointment is quite safely in the past. Your talents are much too varied for you to spend your life carving
wax and pouring hot metal. You are as a son to me; I would
not drive you away with my selfish desires. But to the matter
at hand—" He gave a wry smile. "What *is* the matter at
hand?"

Willan returned the smile. "I need the use of your shop tonight. Tomorrow I go to the Palace as an entertainer—a stage
magician, in fact. You should appreciate the irony. I need to
manufacture certain props."

Mulau tilted his head to one side in a quizzical gesture. "To
the Palace? As a conjurer? When you have the ability to perform true magic? What intrigue are you preparing?"

Willan looked away from the older man. "I cannot tell you
that," he replied. "I can tell you very little at all, I fear. I work
against an enemy of R'thern and it is not likely that you will
see me again after tonight."

Mulau nodded, his suspicions confirmed. "It's a dangerous
business then."

"Yes," said Willan.

"To tell me more would increase the danger?"

Willan nodded. "I may tell you a little more, however. War
impends 'twixt Haldor and R'thern. If it becomes an actuality,
then I will have failed and you should flee R'tha, even if the
forces of R'thern are victorious. Head north or south and

travel as far from the cities as you are able."

Mulau's lips became thin, then he relaxed and sighed. "Well perhaps," he said. "I'll not voice my speculations and I'll promise nothing. In fact, I think that I'll forget that you are leaving and concentrate upon your return." He walked over to a cabinet. "It will be some time before Jon returns and I have a jar of Dragon's Breath that I've been saving. Perhaps this is what I've been saving it for." He poured two cups full of the powerful beverage and handed one to Willan.

"To long life, health, and peace," said Willan, touching his cup to Mulau's. "Have I missed anything?"

"To magic," replied Mulau, and downed his drink with a single swallow.

Chapter Thirteen

Night fell. The past is nearer when darkness lives.

She was in one of the oldest districts of the city, a place of mottled light and patchy darkness. To the unpracticed eye, it would have been difficult to discern which of the buildings were granite and which were of glowstone whose light had faded—whether a particular blotch was caused by age or plaster fill. But she knew.

Nara's journey had begun like a swimmer's tentative entry into turbid waters. As the forcefulness of time had gathered about her, antiquity had yanked her from the safe banks of the moment and submerged her in the past. Images too brief to linger had swirled over her. Here, a lovers' elopement, betrayal and tragedy. There, a jeweled coach of royal splendor, soon to be broken and bare. A narcissistic sorcerer creating a Doppelganger of himself, the only image which he finds worthy of love. War and riot. A drunken brawl, a death, hot aftermath of accusation and recrimination. Parade and protest. Mendacity and sooth. They all swept past, chips on the waves. Vertigo had claimed her; breath came in short gasps of liquid air.

Then the texture of the sensations had changed. The world through which she moved had grown less forceful in its turbulence. The opacity diminished, the swirling clouds evaporated under the tension of her gaze. From murky ocean bottom, she had been transported to the upper air, flying on the currents of time. She soared through canyons of past reality, breathless with the fear and excitement of it but no longer at its elemental mercy. About her fluttered her own past. Sister, cousin to Macou was she, feeling the change winds blow. From the heights she saw:

In the thrice-dimmed past, before magic, before the great architects, before even the nation of R'thern or the self-consciousness of R'tha, there had been a king. He had been a good king, and respected, though much of his circumstance could be traced to good fortune and the lack of calamity during his reign. Even so, late in life he fell prey to the flattery and blandishments of his eldest two sons. The king abdicated in their favor, dividing his kingdom equally between them upon the promise of their care and respect in his retirement. The king had a daughter also, who had married a prince of an outlying district.

The king's sons were cruel, however, and mutually jealous. Their reigns soon grew oppressive and war began. The old king realized his mistake but before he could take action, he was imprisoned and sentenced to die.

His daughter's husband joined the fray and rescued the old king, but at the price of general war. Anarchy flamed and the king's daughter was killed when her capital was besieged and sacked. The king died soon after, of grief.

The great-grandson of the king, Nubogana, grandson of the old king's daughter, grew to maturity as a warrior prince and by blood and conquest fashioned a nation upon the plains of R'thern. And he too was a cruel king, but to his name is added the title Ari, which means "The first great."

Her mother had died when Nara was still a child. Her uncle by marriage, not a gypsy, widowed and childless, became her guardian. They joined one of the semi-permanent camps that existed in the north and he supported the two of them by the cutting and carving of wood. Her uncle had some knowledge (though little talent) at magic. His first instructions to his niece were of the planting of the tree that was to become her staff. She watered it each day and fed her own strength into it through ritual and love. And perhaps because they stayed nearby instead of following the gypsy life, and because there was little else for the young Nara to feed with her attention, the tree flourished and grew straight and sturdy.

Nubogana Ari was only fifteen years old when his father died, leaving him a small demesne beside the river which had survived the general disorders of the time. High-spirited, but lazy and showing no great signs of promise, the boy was known as Domo-Baka, *which means* Lord Fool, *and it was generally assumed that he would be no match for the powerful foes who surrounded him and who coveted his land. In order to bestir him to a proper sense of his responsibilities, his tutor was said to have committed ritual suicide.*

If such an action took place (the deed itself was shrouded in the opacity of violent triumph) it certainly had the desired effect. Far from letting his neighbors help themselves to his lands, Nubogana carried the war into the enemies' territory, with singular success. Before he was thirty, Nubogana had conquered most of central R'thern including the city which became R'tha.

Power eventually went to his head and led to his undoing. In the grounds of the great palace which he had built in R'tha, he constructed a temple in which he himself was to be worshipped. The anger of the gods, some said, was kindled by this impious action. Soon thereafter he was assassinated by Akechi, one of his most trusted generals, whom he had deeply offended by tapping on the head with a fan while in a merry mood.

The Sight had come to her with menarche, and in the beginning its power terrorized her. She would be engaged in simple conversation and phantasms would come. A relative's kiss would open up tapestries of kinship that were smothering in their complexity. She was subject to the dreams and nightmares of those long dead, to the knowledge of fates not yet evident.

Many thought her mad. The Sight had not been so strong for generations. Her contemporaries had only the dimmest and most obscure of visions. Some required drugs or pain to pierce the cloth of everyday reality. Nara was unique and her singularity threatened her sanity.

Her uncle took her away for a time, into the mountains, away from people and their destinies. The slow-moving grandeur of the hills gave her comfort. Her uncle taught her what he knew of magic and of other things. He taught her of the people whom he had known and what he knew of the desires of men, of cities and wars and the way that money flows. Much of his tutelage was unconscious. Her vision stripped him bare before her. He accepted this. It was her supreme good fortune that he had been a man of kindness and wisdom.

Once a week they descended from the hills to water and feed her tree with ritual.

She turned a corner and was confronted with a street of newer buildings, dating from just before the coming of the Demon. A sudden stab of vision came to her from the chaos of the Demon War. A city besieged, the fire pressing to its walls. Only the Five stand against the devil storm:

Within the city the days seemed crystalized, encased. The reservoirs held water for a year. The stores of grain were ample, had been so for as long as any could remember. Famine and drought were strangers to R'tha. As was siege, as was uncertainty, as was fear.

But what if courage should run dry? (A catch of breath, tremor of hands.) Would magic alone suffice? (Cold sweat and nightmared sleep.) Quecora has never before been beaten. (Dry throat and nameless weeping.)

And hopeful reminders: Great Buri has gone into the countryside to raise an army to our cause. The Demon's army starves. Each day subtracts their strength. Each day is added to our benefit. We might still win this game.

It feels so fearful and alone behind these shimmering walls.

A Palace bell gives mournful peal and the Street to Paradise is filled with a waiting throng. Another Guardian of the Towers is carried from the Palace. Five Watchers of the Guards carry yet another body to the hill of graves. There are now but six, the people think. How can they long prevail? And when breaks the Five, do we soon thereafter break as well?

The word comes from the King, his advisors and his Court: Prepare for battle. One way or another, the siege ends soon. Our deliverance or obliteration is soon to be at hand.

Lassitude falls away like moulting feathers. The air fills with the sound of grindstones, the sharpening of swords. One man thinks for all: Just let me near enough to kill a few, he thinks. He gives a brief nod toward the Palace Towers. Just a little longer, please, he thinks. Delay the Demon just a little longer. Let magic answer magic and let me answer steel with steel. He tests the blade against his flesh and grins to see the hint of blood. I'll thresh their bones, he thinks, his angered courage blotting out despair.

Her uncle died when she was eighteen, the year in which she carved her staff from the heart of the living tree. For a time thereafter, she traveled with the Yani, but her spirit was not with them. She was respected and to no small extent feared as well. But there came to her no love or friendship. What attraction may exist between a young woman of willful beauty and the young men who would court her, this attraction could not bridge her instant knowledge of their most private selves. Her power and her scorn estranged her from the world and so she left her kindred to settle into the hills which she could call home.

After the Demon War a revulsion to sorcery sprouted and bore bitter fruit. Kind and gentle men of knowledge were hounded and oppressed. Laws regulating and taxing the practice of magic were instituted. During the worst of the times there were riots and witch hunts, tortures and burnings at the stake. Superstitious fears gave license to the brutes of the street, men of coarse sensibility who craved chaos and were without morality. Such men were drawn toward cruel violence, no matter what their class. They hid themselves in numbers and took pleasures in destruction and pillage. . . .

Two men stood before her. One of them said, "It is not safe for one so beautiful to walk alone through a district such as this."

It required more than an instant for her to affix herself upon the reality of the moment. She had wandered. For hours perhaps. She had—literally—lost all track of time. And place. What place was this? Did her visions substitute for reality or mirror it?

The two men who stood before her did not look like thieves. One was short and fey, with pallid elfin complexion. The other was tall and nearly beardless. Their clothing was fashionable. But for all their exterior refinement, there hung about them an air of decadence indulged. They appeared as gluttons confronted by a feast.

Nara turned to avoid them but they took up positions on either side of her. The short one said, "No, dear lady, you must not leave. It is not safe, do you hear? The streets abound with riffraff." His companion giggled, an unpleasant sound.

"I need not yer company," Nara said and changed her stride. The pair remained beside her, not blocking her path, but at insulting closeness.

"Nonsense, my sweet. Of course you require our assistance and protection. We are known for the quality of our services." His intonation was suggestive and rude. His companion laughed again.

"What would you do," the talkative one continued, "if some lout came up to you and began to take liberties? If someone pressed against you, thus, and caressed you here or here . . ."

She caught his hand in a grip of strength surprising to him. "This," she said in an even tone and her staff touched his hand.

At the contact came his scream. He fell to the ground clutching at his hand.

She whirled to confront her other antagonist, swinging her staff to a position level in front of her. The tall man's eyes were wide and bulging and his arrested stride had left him off balance.

"What? No words of advice?" she inquired mockingly. "No suggestion of the danger should I confront two men intent upon my undoing? Well, let me set yer mind to rest in case ye worry."

She surged forward, her staff catching him mid-chest and pinning him to the wall behind him. She pressed harder. The remaining air in his lungs left grudgingly. He tried to call it back but could not.

"Shall I crush ye like the bug ye are?" she asked. "Or should I stop at punctured lungs and bleeding bile?" She felt the darkness grow within him. She gave one last push and felt a rib crack. His eyes rolled back into his head and he fainted. She shrugged and let him slide unconscious to the ground.

She looked around her. The night glittered, past and present clearly limned and open to her Sight. No apprehension remained. No fear. The heights were hers. She chuckled slightly.

She walked over to the first man who still lay crumpled on the ground, clutching his hand to his bosom and moaning. The skin upon his hand was gray and withered. She knelt and touched his throat. The pain continued, but the moaning ceased.

"Ye've done me a favor of sorts, though it was as unintended as yer fate I'm sure. It's been an entertainment as well. But I must take my leave. However, I'll give to ye a bit of advice. The cost is similar to that of the services that ye proffer.

"The next time that ye seek to obtain favors by theft and force remember this: The hand is not the only extremity that may be withered at a touch." She smiled again and touched his forehead. His breath became even and he slept.

Nara reached up her staff and pulled herself to her feet. Her smile became a feral grin. She raised her hand to cover the moon, shaping its radiance and blotting it from the sky.

Chapter Fourteen

Hiding from the moon, a squat stone building crouched within the fog, flashes of molten brilliance seeping through the cracks in its shuttered windows. Coils of smoke ascended from the chimney on the roof. Occasionally sparks would creep around the conical hood that sat upon the smokespout, to dart and whirl before dancing to oblivion in the mist.

Within the building the wizard worked, his visage in constant shadow even when he stared full face into the open furnace heat. The ring upon his hand pulsed to the furnace's wavering glare and charcoal shimmer of the annealing bowls. The band of darkness which wrapped about his wrist sent shadow tendrils up his arm and shoulder to shield his face from the blinding flames.

At this moment the wizard was hammering a circlet of red hot metal onto a tapered form with a mallet of charred wood. At each blow the metal ring became more nearly matched to the circular cross section of the form, while the mallet head flamed and sparked from the heat and impact. Finally, when he satisfied himself that the ring was as perfectly round as could be judged by human perception, he inverted the form, tapped it once, and the hot metal ring dropped into a bowl of oil and water, which sputtered and boiled at the intrusion.

Willan sighed. It was a tedious task. The rings had to be perfectly round and pleasing to the eye. They were made of steel, for the polish of steel was more impressively solid than that of bronze or brass, and in stage magic appearance was everything. Yet to link the rings required cutting them and then repairing the cut. A shame to breach such workmanship. He shrugged. He used the tongs to remove the ring from the oil and water and held it over a bowl of glowing charcoal. The ring upon his finger grew bright and a thin jet of flame sprang from the charcoal, a flame so hot that its light was nearly invisible. There was a gout of sparks and the ring showed a gap, thin as a fingernail, its edges knife-smooth.

Willan laid the ring aside to return to the forge. Two more strips of iron lay within its hot embrace but he was now concerned with a crucible full of molten brass which had reached the correct temperature. Using the tongs again he lifted the stone cup and stepped over to pour its contents into the casting bed. The fiery liquid filled the cavities left by melted wax. The magician grunted in satisfaction.

In the weeks since he had gained his inheritance, Willan had felt a change begin within himself. At first there had been merely the fumbling beginnings of the known powers of his magic talismans—powers which he had been trained to exercise before he had ever seen the devices. For a time he had thought he understood them. But slowly, as the reality of his heritage had begun to seep into his soul, as his primary understanding had proved inadequate, other changes had begun, changes altogether more subtle and more profound than those which had gone before.

His senses had grown more acute and perceptions came to him of properties not ordinarily observed. He knew instinctively the exact temperature at the heart of the furnace behind him. To merely touch a metal was to know at what heat it melted, its texture, the fluidity of its alloys. He had directly perceived the flow of metal into the casting bed, despite the intervening materials. A glance at a piece of wood or charcoal yielded the knowledge of the potential fire within.

His ring held power in accompaniment to the knowledge. The entire workshop pulsed to his will; heat flowed; flames burnt; elements mingled within the flames, to concentrate and segregate at his command. Fire spoke to him.

The band upon his wrist glowed black and the shadows spoke to him as well, whispering secrets into his inner ear.

They moved about him like a cloak. Once the tongs had slipped and he had grabbed a red hot ingot with his bare hand. The band upon his wrist had gasped and his hand became encased in shadow. His hand had entered shadow, where no heat could reach it. He had not been burned.

Out of habit he still continued to use the tongs, however.

For a moment he stopped. What was that? What had he been thinking? A whisper came. *Out of habit he . . .*

He cocked his head and listened to a silent whisper. He looked over to a worktable where two steel rings lay waiting. He stared at them intently, with eyes in deepest shade.

A puzzled expression on his face, he slowly walked over to the rings and picked them up. He clutched them tightly and blackness grew upon his wrist. His hand grew dark. The ring within the grasp grew dark. He touched the two separated rings together and noted the curious softness of the contact. The lack of sound and hardness. The blackness increased and became something greater than merely the absence of light. He pushed.

He laid the two rings down upon the table. They were now linked together. He walked over to a jug and poured for himself a cupful of water. He drank. Then he laughed, for that was his way, and more than one problem had been solved by the night.

Chapter Fifteen

Britar groaned.

He tried to move without provoking pain. It was not possible. "My head is too large," he muttered and winced at the sound of his own voice.

The thief's shoulders ached, though not with so great a pain as was in his head. His stomach burned. His eyes were still shut tightly; yet through his lids the daylight seemed to be trying to dissolve his skull. This would not be a good thing, he decided, since his head would collapse, his face would fall off and his tongue would slide from his mouth to roll about on the floor. Perhaps it had already done so. How else to explain the taste in his mouth? Yes, his tongue had been on the floor where a herd of giant snails had marched across it, while frogs with pitchforks had jabbed him in the head. From the inside. This seemed as reasonable an explanation as any other. And large ugly men with foul dispositions and heavy boots had kicked his shoulders and back to see if they could penetrate to his stomach. Perhaps they had succeeded, since all of these body parts were complaining angrily.

Britar had drunk wine in Casa, ale in Haldor and mead in Freeland, each with the usual consequences. None of his experiences had prepared him for this. What had he been drinking, anyway? His memory utterly refused to function and all his attempts to concentrate disappeared into a miasma of painful throbs.

Risking terrible consequences, Britar opened one eye. When it did not explode he tried the other as well. Slowly the room came into focus.

Well, whatever I was drinking, he thought to himself, *Its after effects aren't all bad.*

The room was extraordinarily opulent. A heated bathing pool was at its center and wisps of steam swayed in the air above the water. The pool and floor around it were tiled with the finest and most colorful of enamel inlays. Translucent silk curtains hung about the room, offering some degree of privacy to the numerous couches and beds which sat about the perimeter. Above the pool was a stained glass skylight through which wafted light in hues of pink and green and blue. Lesser portals were set at random into the walls and ceiling. Through one of these had come the sunbeams which had awakened Britar.

There were perhaps a score of people strewn about the room in various positions of drunken slumber. Some had obviously lapsed unconscious to the floor; others lay on the huge stuffed couches, singly or in twos or threes or fours. Nearby, Murley the dwarf lay smiling between two splendidly half-dressed women, his legs entwined with one, his head cradled upon the other's breasts.

"Yes," muttered Britar, "I really must find out what I was drinking last night."

"Flamebrew," whispered Murley from his magnificent perch. The dwarf opened one eye and grinned. "Shh," he whispered again as Britar was about to speak. "As I recall, these two," he indicated his female companions, "are best left asleep, since that is practically the only time when they are not talking."

"Part of my problem," whispered Britar in reply, "is that I remember almost nothing of the last night. It is beginning to seem a frightful loss."

"Indeed!" Murley chuckled, then cringed a bit when one of his companions stirred. He continued more softly. "It's a common effect of flamebrew on the novice. The beverage is prepared from the thrice-condensed vapors of aged wine and frozen cider, guaranteed to teach old dogs new tricks and to make young dogs forget them. You yourself put on quite a show while under its effect."

Britar winced. "What did I do?" he asked hesitantly.

"Nothing embarrassing, if that be your worry. You are responsible for our present high estate, I warrant. You were teaching everyone in the bar some Freeland bragging song when a nobleman, a duke, I think, came in. He joined in for a couple of choruses—he'd heard it before, I guess—then we began wagers concerning feats of strength and dexterity. The two of us and the Duke won quite a bit of money."

"How?"

"Well, I climbed a flagpole and danced on it, but that was later. You started things off by undertaking to see how many people could sit on a table with you still being able to lift it."

"Braal," said Britar, thinking of his back and shoulders. No wonder they ached. "How many?" he asked.

"I lost count at six," said Murley with an impish smile. "People kept falling off the table and getting back on again. Anyway, the Duke cleaned up all of the foolish money to be had and we joined his entourage for the night. And here we are. This is his estate."

"Is that all?"

"No, but my memory also fades out somewhere along the line," Murley admitted. He settled back into his fleshy throne. "Besides, it's Carnival, a time for profligacy and fun." He squirmed in pleasure. "This is going to be a good one, I can tell already."

Britar chuckled, but then a scowl crossed his face. "What time is it?" he asked.

"Late morning, I guess," said Murley, squinting at the lights overhead. "Almost noon."

"Ouch!" said Britar as he bolted upright. He shook himself a bit to convince himself that all his body parts were still alive and had not been replaced by wooden imitations. "I promised to meet them at noon." He scrambled to his feet, ignoring his body's protest. Then he stopped short, his gaze meeting Murley's.

Murley smiled. "Till next Carnival, then," he said, the parting phrase to all Carnival friends, evanescent but with a note of genuine warmth and commonality.

"Till next Carnival," said Britar, and he winked. Then he turned to go, stepping over the sleepers 'twixt him and the door.

As he left the chamber Britar heard a brief scuffle behind him. "So you think we talk too much, do you?" someone said testily. Then Murley gave a short exclamation of pain. One of the women had bitten him on the foot.

He ran most of the way to the Palace. Once or twice his flight was transformed from a simple run to a weaving dance when he encountered small parades and found it easier to join the processions than to force his way through. At each step his spirits improved. The exertion relieved him of his ills, the evil humors leaving his body with the sweat. The motion seemed, if not to banish his aches and pains, at least to orchestrate them into manageable proportions. His breathing became easier.

Willan and Nara were waiting for him when he arrived at the appointed place in the great square. The pair stood beside a *crahis*, a small hand-towed cart used in those areas of the city where animal transport was disallowed. Upon the *crahis* were a wooden chest and a burlap bag with bulky contents.

"I hope that I am not late enough to annoy," said Britar as he reached the others. "Have you been waiting long?"

Willan smiled and shrugged. "You came when you were expected," he said with a sidelong glance at Nara. "Come along, it is time for us to make entrance at the Palace."

"Ye should be the one to pull the cart," said Nara to Britar. "Ye are supposed to be our servant, after all." Britar nodded and reached for the handle on the front of the *crahis*.

"What are the contents of the chest?" Britar asked of Willan.

"Magicians' props," replied Willan. "Tools for stage illusions. That within the sack is yours, however."

"Eh?" said Britar. He looked inside the burlap (whose contents were nearly a half barrel in volume). The object within brought a gape to his face. It was a cage of ornamental brass.

"It is an eagle cage," said Willan. "For several years it has been a fad in some quarters to make pets of large birds. This particular cage has a clever locking mechanism. It is triggered by a certain weight upon either of these two perch bars" (he indicated the bars, one inside the cage, one without). "If you set the mechanism for Macou's weight, he may come and go at will."

Britar smiled with delight. "It is much finer than the old cage," he said.

"Fair replacement, nevertheless," said Willan. "Come, let us go to the Palace."

The trio walked across the square to the gates of the Palace. On the flagstones their shadows rippled, foreshortened and shrunken by the hot noontime sun.

"We are Willan of B'ru and the gypsy, Nara, with servant," announced Willan to the keepers of the gate.

The gate was high, and decorated with metal sunflowers in relief, the petals of the flowers triangular and sharp. The gate-keepers stood within the archway of the gate on either side, keeping to the cooler shadows in the heat of the day. One of the keepers carried a sword and was silent. The other man held a board to which various papers were clipped. Behind him were a series of ropes, each a different color.

The man with the papers consulted a list. "Yes," he said. "You are to be conducted to the entertainers' quarters." He pulled on one of the ropes that ran along the wall behind him. In the distance a bell rang, its voice made hollow by the stone hallways.

"You must leave your sword at this gate," the keeper said to Britar. Then he looked at Willan. "The guide will be here momentarily. Will you please unsheath your dagger?"

Willan scowled. "To what purpose?" he asked.

The keeper shrugged. "I'm supposed to examine every blade entering the Palace. Please do not be obstinate."

Willan looked at his companions and sighed. Then he unsheathed D'tias and handed over the blade (which remained small and slender, a dagger instead of a sword).

"Interesting workmanship," the keeper commented.

"An heirloom," Willan replied.

A small portly man appeared from around a corner. "Ah,

guests!" he exclaimed. "Entertainment for the feasts, yes? Here, let me take your things."

With two quick motions he hoisted the chest onto his back and grabbed the sack containing the cage. The small man was stronger than he looked. "Come with me," he said. "I'll show you to your rooms."

As they passed through the entrance from sunlight into shade, Britar looked around at the sharp edges of the metal flowers that decorated the gate. *Now why*, he thought to himself, *do I imagine those as teeth?*

Chapter Sixteen

The baggage carrier informed them that his name was Jever. He jabbered as he led them through the high arched hallways of the great Palace. After reviewing the weather, the previous night's banquets, the state of the Palace, and the quality of the most recent vintages of wine, he said to Nara, "You must be the gypsy that we were told about. You left an impression on Weltan, you did. Scared him a bit, I would say. I'm told that he was so distracted that for hours afterwards he could hardly keep his mind upon his paperwork. But he vouched for you, yes he did. Said that you were the real thing, not some charlatan. So now all the noble ladies want the coins tossed for them, or their palms read, or whatever. Normally they would be more reticent, but it's Carnival! It's all we could do to keep them from your room. But we did! The performers' quarters are for performers' rest and relaxation. Mustn't tire the show people, or they might not give as good a show, eh?"

"I am not particularly tired," said Nara. "Where should I go to greet these ladies of whom ye speak?"

They were at the foot of a stairway. As they started up the stone steps, Jever indicated a hallway to their right. "Down at the end of that corridor are some small meeting rooms. If you wish, I could commandeer one of them for you and I could bring the worthy ladies to you. It would be better for us both that way. You will maintain a higher status if the nobility is made to come to you. For myself, some of the ladies are

known to be generous to those who do them favors—like
helping them to obtain private audiences with a seer."

They had reached the top of the stairs. Jever stopped to
draw a deep breath, slightly winded. He said, "But then, being a seer, you know these things already."

"Yes," said Nara, and she strode down the hallway to open
a door and enter their quarters. The little man looked after
her, a faint scowl touching his face as he realized that he had
not told her which door was the correct one.

Willan decided to use the afternoon for sleep. Britar, realiz-
ing that he had not eaten all day, asked Jever the directions to
food. The little man complied.

Despite the directions, Britar soon became lost in the im-
mense Palace. If truth be told, he prefered it thus, to use the
opportunity and the excuse for exploring the antiquarian
splendor of the Palace of the King's Light. He passed through
galleries of hanging tapestries and frescoed walls, conference
rooms, meeting halls, and great corridors finely paneled with
aged wood, carved and polished. He encountered numerous
denizens of the Palace, some queerly dressed in the manner of
outlanders, or entertainers, or religious disciples. Others
were servants, or carried themselves with the hauteur of nobility, or walked with the languid *come to me* of the courtesan. But this was Carnival and appearances were deceptive.
Who could say if that woman who appeared a slattern was
not really a nobleman's wife, or a widow casting aside the
mourning veil, or an acolyte of some sect performing a bizarre penance?

From time to time he encountered a cul de sac and had to
retrace his steps. Or else he entered a restricted area and was
redirected by guards. After perhaps an hour's wandering,
when some of the corridors were beginning to seem familiar,
he came to the banquet halls and the great courtyards beyond.

The courtyards were at the very center of the Palace, forming the inevitable five-sided figure in their configuration. The
banquet halls were the innermost rooms of the building, and
extended into the open spaces of the courtyards to form pa-

tios and terraces. For Carnival the courtyards had been turned into a giant outdoor kitchen. Deep pits had been dug and hot charcoal fires glowed within them. Over the coals hung whole steers, boars, and giant poultry, all slowly roasting in the heat. Buried in the coals were yams and vegetable clusters encased in clay. When they were done, they would be removed with tongs, the clay coverings would be cracked open and the delicacies within consumed. Teams of servants worked with flashing knives at long wooden tables slicing fruits and leafy vegetables into fragments which slid down the tables into enormous salad bowls at the end.

Britar surveyed the scene for several moments and noted a pretty servant girl seated on the ground next to a table upon which rested a large cask of wine. He approached her to say, "I know that the question appears stupid, given the surroundings, but how might I procure something to eat?"

She grinned at him, leaped to her feet and scurried off, saying, "Wait right there," over her shoulder. In a moment she returned with a fowl's leg and an empty mug. She handed him the meat and filled the mug with wine from the cask. The two of them then seated themselves upon the ground. She handed him the wine.

"Usually I work as a serving girl during the banquets," she explained. "I am only helping out here as a favor to a friend, so I'm allowed a longer rest break than the others. But just you wait. Soon the head man will begin to scowl and it's back to work for me." She grinned at Britar. "He'll probably leave me alone though until he ascertains whether or not you are of high station."

"My status is fairly low," Britar admitted. "Still I am grateful for the aid and company. All meals should be so pleasant."

She smiled at the compliment. "Are you one of the entertainers?" she asked.

"I am squire to one of them," replied Britar. "I travel with a magician."

"Ah, that sounds exciting," she said, and Britar could not disagree. "Do you get to travel to many places?"

"I have been with him for only a short time, but yes, we travel. I was something of a vagabond before I came into my present position. I have seen most of the western lands and many of those to the north. R'thern was one of the few places still completely unknown to me, and Willan—that is the magician's name—suggested that Carnival was a good time to see R'tha."

"He is right," she said earnestly. "There is nowhere so grand as R'tha in Carnival.

"Still," she said wistfully, "I would like to travel some day. My fiance is a soldier and he has promised me that when he becomes an officer and we wed, then we'll travel widely. He already moves about more than I like to think about, but I would not mind if he could take me with him."

"We saw bands of soldiers heading north when we came to the city. There does seem to be a lot of movement lately. And much building of fortifications."

"Yes," she said. "Perhaps Roal was among those you saw. He left but a few short days ago. He could not tell me where he was going, but his leaving was all in a rush. All my friends say that there is to be war with Haldor. If that is so, Roal will win promotions rapidly and we might be married within the year."

If he lives, thought Britar sourly, but he withheld the thought. "So R'tha revels on the eve of war. Pleasure before the danger. There is poetry in that. It lends spice to the gaiety."

She waved her hand in dismissal. "Fear of war or fear of boredom, it is all the same. Each takes from Carnival what each brings to it. I'm sure that the gods of the feast are too ancient to be aroused by a little war." She looked around. "I have a little while yet before the head man begins to scowl, so tell me of the places that are the farthest from here."

So Britar told her truths and lies in equal proportion and many times she took the fable as veracity and scoffed at faithful accounts of happenings that he had seen.

It took him less time to return to the entertainers' quarters than it had taken him to find the courtyards. He was beginning to understand the hallways of the Palace.

When he arrived back at the rooms he found Willan still

asleep. For a time Britar amused himself with the examination of the cage that Willan had given him. The locking mechanism in particular fascinated him. A push on the exterior bar, firm and exact, like so, and a *click whirr* opened the cage. Less pressure and there was no effect. More pressure than was required to open the cage and the bar slipped to a lower position and locked. Ease the pressure once again and the bar moved up and found the opening sequence. *A marvel*, thought Britar.

Willan groaned and rolled to a seated position on the bed, rubbing his face and yawning. Britar left the cage where it sat. He walked over to seat himself on a chair across from Willan's bed.

"Would you hand me that jug?" asked Willan, indicating a stone container on the table next to Britar. Britar handed Willan the jug, which was filled with water. The wizard drank greedily.

"Have you been exploring the Palace?" Willan asked after wiping his mouth on his sleeve.

"Indeed I have," said Britar. "The place resonates with desperate gaiety." He related to Willan his conversation with the serving girl, and the rumors of impending war.

"The noose grows tight," mused Willan. "We do not have much time in which to act."

"We may have even less time than we fear," said Britar. "Events move more swiftly than I would have believed possible."

"He is right," said Nara, entering the room. Her face had a masklike quality to it. She closed the door behind her, walked across the floor and sat down beside Willan on the bed. She spoke in a quiet voice, almost a whisper, as if to guard against being overheard. Her voice had a measured cadence. "The presence of Quecora permeates this place. The stench of him is dense upon the dwellers here. The merest glimpse of their lives shows knots of intrigue."

She stopped and blinked, then her face curved in a bare smile. "Pardon me," she said. "I've been telling too many fortunes today and my speech is artificial and strange." She paused and sighed. Then she continued in a more natural tone, "Briefly what I have learned is this: there is to be a war, and soon, perhaps within the fortnight. This much is clear from the questions which those foolish women put to me. 'Will my Saun be safe?' one asked. Or 'When will Humphar return? Will he be faithful while he is gone? Will his injuries be minor?' And so forth. Concern for position, safety and fidelity. The usual notions, but so intense as to be embarrassing.

"I think that the war is to have the double purpose of subduing Haldor and killing off the Demon's opposition here in R'thern, unwitting though that opposition may be. King Seilung's death was murder. We knew that already. His son, Tilwesser, the new King, is easily swayed by flattery and is susceptible to dreams of military glory. The King's Council numbers ten, and any one of them could be a Demon thrall. Or none of them. Each council member has a large staff and an agent there could be nearly as influential as anyone in the council."

"Who do you suspect?" asked Willan.

"No one, everyone. It doesn't matter, don't ye see? Quecora's web is too complex. He touches a strand here for a movement over there. The murder was done by his witting agent, I am sure. But I think that it was done in order to shift power amongst those who have no knowledge of what is to be.

"When the Demon comes to power it will not be through control of the present leaders. All will be smashed eventually and remade. His present manipulations are to set the stage for later action. The State and its laws will be recast in another image. But even then the Beast may not show himself directly. He is far more cunning now than centuries ago. His goals also may have changed. Perhaps . . ." her voice trailed off.

"Go on," said Willan.

She glanced toward the window, toward the impending dusk. "There are many religions in R'tha, new ones every year. Perhaps he no longer wishes to rule so much as he wishes to be worshipped."

There was silence in the room for a time, which each of the trio imagined the horrors contained in this possibility. Gods were known to be even crueler than kings.

Best not to think of such things, thought Britar. So he spoke to break the silence. "You said that the old King was murdered by the Demon's agent. Can you not discover who this is?"

"And go for a brief stroll in Hell besides?" she mocked. "Ye cannot know how dangerous clairvoyance is in this place. The seer may be seen as well. To be caught spying on Quecora . . ." She shuddered. "It is not for nothing that no gypsies have been here lately. This Palace reeks of danger. Others with Sight less clear than my own would not know the source of their fear, but they would avoid approaching the Palace. They would probably avoid R'tha altogether. Perhaps they are wiser than we."

She looked at the two men. "I will get only one chance to penetrate this web. I wish for it to be fruitful and I shall be as cautious as I am able. I have no wish to die here. But I am no longer optimistic about our chances. I have arranged with those I saw this afternoon to perform a trysting tonight at midnight. It will be well attended; even some council members will be there if their wives are to be believed. Perhaps even the King will attend.

"From the trysting, perhaps, if all goes well and if we escape with our lives, I hope to obtain a *geis.* A *geis* is a . . . construct, similar to a tryst ghost but more permanent and without physical form or will. It may be represented by an image or even a phrase of prosody. That is its key. Within the *geis,* obtained by meditation upon the key, will be knowledge of Quecora and his plans. But the *geis* is a thing in itself; it will not be a part of Quecora. It will thus be safe, or at least as safe as any knowledge can be. Maybe it will tell us how to defeat the Demon." She slumped in her chair and placed a hand upon her cheek. "Please tell me a better plan. The odor of this place has worn on me. I wish that we could leave."

Willan compressed his lips and shook his head from side to side. "I know of no other plan," he said. "But I may be able to relieve some of the risk. Or at least I may be able to draw some of the danger away from your actions." He leaned forward to tell her of his thoughts.

Chapter Seventeen

A Carnival banquet in the Palace of Light: the most festive occasion within the grandest habitation in the world's supreme metropolis. The very air shimmered with delight.

Within the central courtyards, bonfires blazed, and citizens danced amid the pungent aromas of the food cooking in the firepits. The musicians played the fashionable dances, which went to a rhythm midway between a march and a heartbeat. Large casks of wine and ale spilled their contents into waiting mugs and thence into gaping mouths. Laughter brayed and echoed from stone to sod.

The gatherings within the Palace divided, none too neatly, into dining and entertainment. There was much mingling of the two functions. Singers and storytellers circulated in the banquet halls, while some of the nobles took their meals in private boxes within the auditoriums wherein the stage acts and theatrical endeavors were displayed.

One of the theaters was given exclusively to the presentation of stage illusion, and it was here that the new King took his dinner, for he had a fondness for prestidigitation and was a dabbler in the art himself. So it was in this hall, before assembled royalty and many of the King's Court, that Willan presented himself and his skills.

In contrast to his afternoon performance he now kept silent. There was intermittent noise from beyond the hall, drunken song or drumming from the courtyard and interior rooms. Many of the nobles within the hall continued to eat their meals. But soon the attention of the gathering became firmly affixed upon the tall wizard's actions.

A hooded brazier touched his movements with a light smoke, tinted by various candles whose illumination changed in color as the candles burned. Willan's flowing garments swirled about him as he moved, also changing hue in counterpoint to the candlelight and obscuring his actions in the time-honored manner of magicians.

Willan's first offering was the Monrovian Loop Illusion, which he followed with the Sixth Night Trick. Seldom had the assembly seen a smoother performance of either of these. Then the Gyrator of VanJac brought forth gasps of astonishment as the fiery jewels blazed merrily while dancing above the stage. The Box of a Thousand Songs then called forth tears of nostalgia from those still susceptible to memories of youth. But before those tears were fully dry, they were joined by cries of laughter and delight at the Worthy String with the Chain of Straw Variations, inanimate objects moving in patterns both silly and profound.

The candles sputtered; all died save two which had turned to a hue of deepest azure. Willan then performed a special treat: Twelve Memories and a Bubble, which involves little illusion but much in the way of atmosphere and mood. All motion within the auditorium ceased and the audience was transfixed.

The last memory faded and the bubble burst, leaving a cloud of silken scarves to flutter to the floor. A few fell onto the small magician's table in front of Willan. He smiled and gathered them into a pile. As he waved his arms above the scarves, the heap of silk shivered and began to grow. It became apparent that the scarves had quilted together into a single cloth which rose as if pushed upward from below. Willan snatched the cloth away to reveal a hookah made of ivory and newly cast brass, which gleamed red and green in the shifting light of the two remaining candles.

Willan waved the silks above his head. Flame sprouted in his grasp and arched downward with his motion to light the hookah in the final blazing instant. He picked up the hookah stem and drew a puff of smoke. There was applause. He blew a smoke ring which went from red to green to black as it passed through the candles' light into the darkness over the heads of the crowd.

He blew again and swirled his robe to disperse the ring just as it passed beyond the final candle's light. The candles sputtered more frequently now, and the hoops of smoke weaved through several color changes before vanishing at the wizard's wave. Turquoise, scarlet, magenta, and mauve, all danced and changed and disappeared.

The light became blue-gray and silvery and Willan blew another ring. Just before the darkness claimed it, he reached out and flicked at it with his finger. There was a quiet *ting*, as if at the sounding of a tiny bell, and then Willan's other arm again swirled the ring into oblivion.

As the next ring reached the spot where all the rest had vanished, Willan swooped his arm in front of it, snatching at the air. There was another *ting* and Willan now held a ring of hard and gleaming steel within his grasp. There was applause.

He blew another ring of smoke and again caught a bright metal band. He clinked the two of them together to demonstrate their solidity, then tossed one lightly into the air, where it seemed to hang for an instant longer than gravity would allow. Willan reached the other ring up as he caught the first. The two rings were now linked.

Willan blew another ring, caught it, then linked it silently to the others. He slipped the three ring chain onto his right arm. He produced two additional rings, catching the second upon the first in the same motion with which he transformed them from smoke to metal. He looped these over his left arm, and slipped the three rings from his right. He blew and caught another ring, spinning it in his hand and joining it to the chain of three. He passed it up and down the chain, silently, as if the rings were still fashioned out of smoke. He removed the two rings from his left arm and snatched two more rings from smoke to add them.

The metal chains now became alive as they danced within the wizard's grasp. They levitated, separated, branched and rejoined. Rings passed up and down and through the chains, silently for the most part, or occasionally making a bell-like *ting*. Sometimes they left his grasp completely and floated in front of him, shimmering on the air. The light from the candles flickered and none could tell if there might be, perhaps, just perhaps, thin black threads manipulating the rings. None cared. The beauty of the rings brought a lump to the throat.

Slowly then, as the rings still danced, Willan began to remove them from their bondage. The first he tossed to the audience. A nobleman caught it, banged it once to prove it solid, then led a round of applause. The second ring to be removed hovered for a moment in front of Willan and he banished it with a swirl of his cape. A small puff of smoke marked its passing.

Next Willan removed two rings, still linked, and tossed them to the crowd. Then he banished several more to smoke and tossed another pair to the front of the stage where they spun merrily and were snatched up by front row onlookers.

There were now three rings within Willan's grasp and a certain tension filled the room. Some of the onlookers, those well-versed in stage illusion, had been able to follow the performance and knew these three rings to be solid steel, unbreached by the small gap required for the trick of the linking rings. Willan smiled. Unnoticed by all, the band upon his wrist grew dark, as his hand became a thing of shadow. The guttering candles grew dark and a light of royal purple spread through the room.

The rings hovered in front of him, suspended on the threads between his hands. A sudden jerk and the steel bands leaped skyward; Willan's hand darted to the middle ring and pulled it to him. Into shadow. Through the darkness of the immaterial, untouching and untouched by the other rings. With a sweep of his left hand he caught the two remaining rings upon their downward path and extended the sweep into a low bow. The candles went out, plunging the hall into darkness. In the next instant the torches blazed forth as did the applause of the assembly. Willan bowed low once more, straightened and handed the three rings to an usher who carried them to the box of the King. Willan bowed again as all within the hall, led by the King, rose in their ovation. More bows, then Willan left the stage.

The sound of the applause followed him. The ring upon his hand throbbed its warning.

Behind the stage was a passageway that led to the entertainers' dressing rooms and thence to a greeting room set aside for the performers and those wishing to pay them praise. When Willan arrived here after having stored his equipment, Britar and Nara were already waiting for him.

"Excellent. Flawless," said Britar. "The audience loved it."

"I thought it properly performed as well," said Nara and she embraced the wizard. She whispered in his ear, "In the last moments of yer act, the Demon's stench grew very strong. Ye have his attention now. Be careful."

Willan stepped back, still holding her hands. "I am sure that your efforts tonight will also meet with success." He smiled and winked at her. "I think that I am about to be beset with fans."

He spoke correctly. A dozen or more well-wishers crowded around him. Nara and Britar dropped back to watch the scene. Willan smiled, shook hands, laughed and joked—the very image of the successful entertainer.

After many minutes the crowd thinned and a spare, dark-haired man approached Willan. "Your name is Willan, is it not? I am told that you are from the southern hill country. My name is Hoxa. I am aide to finance minister Zogu."

The two men shook hands and with the contact, Willan's ring finger tingled slightly. He stole a glance at Nara. She nodded imperceptibly, then motioned to Britar to follow her as she left the room.

The two men exchanged pleasantries, Hoxa praising Willan's performance and Willan graciously accepting the praise.

"Southerners are purported to be the master magicians," said Hoxa. "It is even said that some of the old skills still survive among the clans, that remnants of true magic remain."

"We do nothing to discourage the belief," admitted Willan. "There may even be some truth to it. Some clan bloodlines may be traced back to the Toltan sorcerer kings, or so I have been told. A few ancient texts survive in obscure languages and poor translations. I have seen a few of these, but I know little of their use. They seem somehow incomplete, as if the language used was more allegorical than exact."

"Ah, well put," said Hoxa. "I myself have seen such fragmentary texts and have been perplexed by them as well. How does one mix three knoles of brutish with two drabs of night, when brutish is extinct, knoles are an unknown quantity, and the night refuses to enter a drabspoon but instead persists in filling the time between sunset and dawn?"

Willan laughed and observed that the endeavor might prove difficult.

"Still," continued Hoxa. "You've a real talent for the stage, and some of your tricks are very well done. I know that prying secrets from magicians is as easily accomplished as filling a drabspoon with moonlight, but maybe I can tempt you away to a private conversation. I have a few of those texts of magical lore within my working quarters, which by happenstance are not far from here. Would you care to see them?"

Willan said, "My kinsmen would never forgive me if I passed up the opportunity."

"Then follow me," said Hoxa.

With the passage of time and the dimming of the glowstone, night now penetrated more deeply into the Palace than at the time of its design. Of course the sleeping quarters had been built of dark granite, but for many centuries the hallways of the King's abode had never known a torch, for the walls themselves provided adequate light. Not so now, however; and providing smokeless torches and candles to the Palace was a flourishing enterprise.

The finest torches were comprised of a mixture of fiber, beeswax, and the naptha which bedewed certain interior caverns of the eastern mountains. Sometimes essential oils were added to the compounds to achieve an airy scent: fresh flowers or cedar or pine.

During Carnival, lighted candles served two purposes: as illumination, either singly or in chandeliers, and for the keeping of time. All winding of clocks was banned during Carnival, so marked candles served as timepieces during the night when sundials were useless. This banning of clocks had been a major exercise of political skill by the candlers guild some six score years previous.

In the room which had been set aside for Nara's use, most of the candles in the chandelier had been extinguished. The few remaining would provide dim light when the trysting began. Before that time torches still burned along the walls of the room as the crowd milled about inside. Nara and Britar stood at the doorway, preparing to make their entrance.

"I am not certain about what will happen here tonight," Nara told Britar. "So I cannot warn ye of the possible dangers. Just mingle with the crowd and try to look efficient. Yer supposed to be my helper and ye are certainly that. I may probe more safely through ye than I could by myself. Here." She propped her staff beside the door, then touched Britar's chest and forehead with light fingers.

Do not speak, came her voice though her lips remained still. *Just nod if ye can hear me.* Britar masked his surprise and nodded.

Good. I must take the measure of all who join the trysting and fit them together smoothly. Ye will help. Speak to the people. Shake their hands, touch their shoulders, brush them as they pass. Ye are my touch. For safety's sake I must confine myself to my eyes and ears.

They entered the room.

"Lady Kanti," said Nara warmly. "How good of ye to come. And ye brought so many of yer friends. There is not room for everyone at the table, I fear, but all may watch. This promises to be quite an evening."

Nara bowed low and Britar did the same. She continued, "This is my associate Britar of Freeland, a man of considerable resource and strength of will. He is to be our anchor as we sail the oceans of the spirits."

· *My, she spreads it deep and wide*, thought Britar. Then he felt a small kick though no one had touched him. *Mustn't second-guess a professional*, came Nara's voice from inside his head. *I don't tell ye how to pick a purse. Now go and introduce yourself to Lady Iol and her husband Saun. She is the one in green.*

Britar complied. He moved through the gathering at Nara's directions, smiling, kissing the hands of the ladies, firmly grasping those of the men. His skills as a pickpocket aided him in his task; he could slide through a crowd unobtrusively, barely touching anyone, yet still making contact. The channel between him and Nara widened and he fancied that he could hear the murmur of her thoughts, along with the babble of conversation in the room.

The blonde woman over there has recently taken a lover, the young man in the purple cape. They ignore each other from across the room. The woman's husband is boring and trivial, but obviously high placed. People listen to his words with ambition and contempt. Go meet him, Brit. I need his name. Ah, Onrie. Good.

"Lady Jedith," said Nara. "Would ye be the first to sit at our table?" She led the chosen one to the large circular table off to one side of the room. "And you, Lord Ur, will ye sit beside her? The trysting circle requires alternating man and woman, for harmony. The group personality must be balanced." Lord Ur took his seat.

That young officer is fearful of death. A darkness hangs about him; his fear may bring about its own reality. More hints of war. Damn and double damn.

Over there. Two women, both of whom appear to be, shall we say, lacking in intelligence? For that one the appearance is an imposture. She shows perception in an occasional glance and this betrays her. She has a buried sadness, too deep to safely probe, and old. Her companion needs no artificial vacuity. The blankness runs deep. Which do we need? Perception or a buffer? Cast caution to the wind. Seat the first.

"Hello, my name is Aloquere." Britar kissed her hand.

There came Nara's voice. *Seat her next to Jurla or Morgane.*

"Will you follow me?" asked Britar. "We would like your presence in the circle." He smiled at Aloquere's companion as if to say, "Sorry, better luck next time."

The babble of voices stopped.

The King had entered the room, accompanied by guards and sycophants. Nara approached him and bowed.

"Sire," she said. "Yer presence does us great honor. So strong a force as yerself would tend to unbalance the circle, yet I will try to compensate if ye are of a mind to join us. Or ye may watch our humble doings from the side and thereby enrich the proceedings with yer attention."

Tilwesser smiled at the flattery. "We have no wish to dominate. Not during Carnival. We will watch and learn."

Nara smiled. "Then may I borrow one of yer men to complete the circle? That he may report on his experience to ye?" The King nodded and Nara guided a startled guard to the table, after handing his sword to another of the King's men for safekeeping.

The time was nearly midnight.

Chapter Eighteen

A cat watched them from the shadows, its eyes flickering with the light of the single torch that lit the corridor. The small beast prowled the halls where the solemn business of state was conducted, halls unused during Carnival, removed from the gaiety. Only cats moved in the dimly lit passages. Only cats and other creatures of the night.

"Here we are," said Hoxa, turning a lock with his key. "My humble workspace." The door swung open. He pulled a cord and a veil fell from a crystal globe of glowstone, recently quarried and therefore of considerable rarity and brilliance. Light spilled forth to fill the outer office and reached into the room beyond.

Hoxa had spoken with irony. His rooms were spacious and luxuriously furnished, well deserving the security of the locked door. (No easy task to breach that lock, Willan reflected.) Hoxa was obviously a man of considerable stature and influence.

"It seems commodious enough to serve as a residence," Willan commented.

"There is a third room which you cannot see from here," said Hoxa. "Some bureaucrats, upon attainment of the third, do just that, move into the Palace permanently, and shun the rabble outside. They become like slugs beneath a rock, torpid and bloated with themselves. I'll not be snared that way. Bad enough to work here. To dream here? Ugh! But let me show you my prizes."

The outer office contained a desk and library. The books were an assortment of legal volumes, ledgers, military texts, maps, and other reference works. Hoxa unmasked another crystal to reveal the softer furnishings of the second room. There were several comfortable chairs and footstools; two tables, upon one of which rested a chessboard. A winerack stood off to one side. The walls were decorated with paintings, woodprints, and several niches holding metal sculptures. Hoxa pointed to one of these. The bronze figure of a woman danced within the niche, sword aloft, drinking a demon's blood. "The goddess of death from an ancient religion," said Hoxa. "Do you know the myth?"

Willan nodded. He knew the statue as well. It had brought bad luck to Juba, its sculptor. He had badly burned his hand in the casting of it. His shop had been lost to a fire the day before the statue's sale. Only this one metal figurine had survived the conflagration; Juba's apprentice, his son, had not. The sculptor had sold the statue the next day and had killed himself the day after that. Willan hid his shudder and turned away, pretending interest in an abstract work which hung upon the wall.

"That was made by a process similar to woodcut printing," said Hoxa. "A wax is painted over a porous piece of flat bark and only the uncovered portion retains the ink."

As Hoxa continued his discourse, Willan found himself both attracted and repelled by the character of his host. Hoxa's demeanor was smooth and amiable. The furnishings of his room further bespoke a man of breeding and taste. But there was an undercurrent of cynicism to the man that found release in isolated remarks of cutting sarcasm. Willan wondered about the inner man; nor did he forget Nara's warning.

"Ah, but I did not bring you here to boast of my possessions. I hope to pick your brain a bit as well." He indicated one of the chairs. "Wait here. I'll get those texts of which I spoke."

He produced another key and went to the door of the third room. From his chair, Willan could catch no more than a glimpse of the room beyond, then the door swung shut. His brief sight had included a workbench filled with various apparatus, retorts, flasks, spinwheels, and crucibles. And was that obscure object a human skull?

The torches had been extinguished; only the sparse candle-light from the chandelier lit the room. The brightness was that of moonlight and shadows. On the great round table a single brazier burned, emitting heat but no light.

Nineteen people sat at the table while Nara stood at her place. She was nearest to the wall, her back but a few feet from the stone. Britar sat to her left.

She nodded to the crowd of people who stood against the wall on the other side of the room. The King of R'thern smiled at her.

She produced a small vial and poured oil into the brazier. A dim flame appeared over the hot coals. The flame burned with a rolling flicker which seemed always to be on the verge of going out entirely.

Nara sat down and took the hands of the two men at her sides. "Make a ring," she told the gathering. Forty hands clasped to form a circle.

"It would not do to be too precise in yer expectations," she told them. "Each trysting is singular; uncertainty and surprise are essential ingredients in the spiritual formulation. Still, some features are common to many trystings, in the same way that different dreams by different dreamers often contain common elements. That is how ye may view a trysting if ye like, as a shared dream, where fantasy and fact may meet, and where hallucination is not always a private matter. Ye will probably be given sight of some of yer fears and hopes and desires and those other things which ye share with yer neighbors. More than that I dare not predict.

"So clear yer minds of distractions, as if ye were preparing for sleep. Keep the circle no matter what ye may see or hear or think. Be not surprised or fearful in yer conscious mind at what is about to transpire. Yer dreams are about to be shown to ye and then who knows what may happen? For yer dreams are the greatest power ye possess."

She nodded at the dim-flamed brazier which rested at the center of the table. "There sits our gateway," she said. "The

center of our common dreams. Watch its light and listen with
me."

She then began to speak in a voice that was not quite a
chant, not quite a song, but still was sonorous and sweet. The
language was archaic and arcane, beyond the memory of any
in the room. Nara's quiet voice filled the room, and all who
heard began unconsciously to breathe in time to its rhythm:

> *Atau reau taur ryda lam*
> *Paday Sinthi ai'*
> *Wa'an de te heau cula' aram*
> *For wa'an tich radi ai'*
> *Oni ai*
> *Adi ai . . .*

Britar stared at the dim red flame that swayed at the center
of the tryst circle. Its motion was pleasant, soothing. He felt
the muscles of his scalp and abdomen relax. He had not even
realized his tension until it vanished. A warmth suffused his
body, flowing through his limbs like the slow roll of the flame
before his eyes.

As he watched, he began to see subtle variation in the col-
oration of the burning vapors. Within the red were hints of
orange and umber that moved more quickly than the overall
motion of the flame. Mites of yellow sparks and black soot
swarmed with near invisibility about the brazier top.

In the space between the rapid darting of the sparks and the
slow sway of the flame, there beckoned reverie. The shapes
before his eyes suggested memories forgotten and old desires
rekindled. The lassitude which had claimed his body grew
thick and a pleasant buzzing filled his head. He sighed and
was not surprised when the exhalation was in unison with
others in the circle.

Warmth brushed his forehead and he remembered his
mother's touch. Her face briefly swirled within the flame.
Then a touch of phantom lips came as he glimpsed the face of
his first love. The image was gone before he could blink. A
contraction of his stomach brought forth images of meat pies
and ale. His nostrils filled with the illusory scent of them. The

woman directly across the table from him licked her lips.

Warmth briefly caressed his loins and he felt a stab of desire so intense that he nearly choked; the flame presented a scene of unparalleled eroticism. He blinked and the image became that of mountain snows and hyacinths. He gave thanks for the dim light for he suspected himself to be blushing.

His memory became confused. Whence came that image of cliffs and fog? Had he ever been atop such a mountain peak? A wolf howled just below his hearing and he felt the circle grow taut. The fear dissolved into laughter as the brazier flame sprouted a clown's face. Then slowly the makeup peeled away and his own face stared back. He blinked and the image subtly changed. Another blink, another mutation. Various aspects of himself slipped by, too swift to analyze. At intervals, others' faces came to him, the faces of those seated about the circle. There came a merging, a melding. He stared into a face that was recognizably his own, yet which contained aspects in common with the other tryst members. Another transition. He recognized the face of the one called Aloquere. She seemed entranced. Her expression was similar to that which had been upon his own image but a moment before.

Nara spoke. "The circle has chosen an emissary." She paused. "Aloquere?"

"Yes?" replied the young woman. Her voice was that of one near sleep.

"How do ye feel?" asked Nara.

"Warm. Light. So light that I could float, I think. If only the ceiling were not so low I could perhaps even fly."

"The ceiling is but a material barrier. It cannot stop ye. If ye hold onto us we can give ye wings. Would ye like that?"

"Oh yes."

"Very well then. Close yer eyes. Ye are very light now. Let us make ye lighter still. There are no ceilings where ye are going. Ye are lighter than a feather. There is only open space before ye. Ye can fly with the birds. Ye are lighter than the air. Lead us now.

"Fly," said Nara.

Into the spaces between the worlds, young Aloquere

spread her wings.

Willan pored over an ancient text, bound in animal skin, its pages trimmed in gold. His father's study held a similar volume, but the one that he now held was newer and in the language of the North rather than in the Toltan tongue. There had been revisions as well. In the section on transmutation, for example, certain of the alchemical formulae had been transposed and substitutions had been made. Willan doubted that the alterations would have any effect upon the efficacy of the procedures involved; they would not work in either case. The sorceries involved had been impotent for centuries.

Willan pretended engrossment while he tried to assess his situation. His fire ring tingled in warning. It was past midnight; the trysting had begun. He was now in the lair of Hoxa, who was surely in the Demon's thrall. He must keep his host preoccupied, lest the Demon be alerted through the perceptions of his henchman. But how?

Willan closed the text and said, "An interesting work, but I doubt its utility. Some of my people have attempted the use of similar formulae, but to no avail. It has been suggested that there is a missing ingredient: the 'Substance Metaphysique,' which will make the conjurations effective. My father, on the other hand, believed that the language of power has shifted in semantics, so that it no longer reflects reality. This would suggest that the spells should be translated into modern usage but with the ancient meanings. If this is true, I consider it to be a hopeless task."

"I have an alternate hypothesis," said Hoxa.

"Yes?"

"As you indicate, the least effective spells are those which involve the use of language as the controlling factor. Perhaps the commands are the same but there is no longer anyone or anything to be commanded."

"You are suggesting that the spells invoke entities which no longer exist?"

"Exactly," said Hoxa. "I believe that the age of powerful spirits is past. There are no more demons."

At the last word Willan's ring gave a throb so forceful that he nearly winced. With an effort he shrugged and turned to gaze at Hoxa's chessboard. "That is an interesting theory," he said. "I will have to ponder it."

"Do you play?" asked Hoxa.

"Eh?"

"Chess," said Hoxa. "Do you play chess?"

Willan looked at his host and smiled. The chessmen before him were like old friends. He had made several similar chess sets. He probably knew the man who made this one.

"Yes," said Willan. "I play chess."

Chapter Nineteen

The circle has chosen an emissary.

The words of the dark lady still linger in my ears. *Fly,* the gypsy said. Oh, I can. Oh, I do.

Down below I see the city's glow—so pale from such a height. I dream that I play tag with fragile clouds. They feel cool against the mind, like thoughts of mint and mountain breezes. I float to follow fancy and wild impulse.

Mountain breezes. Dense clouds to the north and west.

There will be no rain for our western regions. Not for many weeks. The water beneath the earth cries out in vain to its cloud brother. The sky flickers red in portent. Why? The circle bids me nearer. I fly to the northwest with the speed of dreams.

There are wagons on the road; the army moves and fortifies. Wagons on a hill and steep incline. I see a wagon dragged back by its load. There are corpses in this wagon, corpses from the fighting yet to come. The spokes burst out of the wagon wheels and the bodies spill into the dirt. The drivers of the other wagons remove their axletrees to avoid a similar fate. All motion ceases.

There! Running! A pig covered with dirt! The corpses become devils that snarl at the moon. A harness breaks and the horse and wagon part. The horse runs into the forest. The demon driver cries bloody tears as he beats a drum.

The team horse goes astray.

Into the forest he runs. The horse becomes a deer. I have no woodsman guide; the way may be lost. The mist rises.

The circle will provide.

The mist swirls, forming scenes before my eyes. Footprints crisscross in the snow. There lies a tied-up sack. It contains a box.

Do not open it. Move on.

I see a field. Foxes in amid the sheep. At the center of the meadow stands a pole with writhing snakes. The sheep become dragons and fall upon the foxes. Now the dragons fight. Their blood is black and yellow. The last one dies calling to me with my mother's voice.

From the body of the dragon comes a tortoise, now two, now ten. They plod about a pool of water. I hold a mirror in my hand, a mirror rimmed with tortoise shell.

What do ye see in the mirror?

I see . . . a jug of wine and a bowl of rice. Fish in a tank. A knife alongside an axe. I pour wine into a goblet and give it to my companion. He is the stocky one, the helper to the gypsy.

We drink. My companion smiles. I walk to the window and gaze out onto the courtyard below. A prince shoots a hawk that perches upon a high wall. The bird dies and is devoured by butterflies. There is a gate in the wall.

Gates are to be opened.

It opens onto a narrow street. A bronze statue of a man stands to one side. The curtain of a passing carriage drops free and the woman within sits transfixed by the man of bronze. Her finery turns to rags. Nearby, a man chained within stocks begins to laugh. His feet are not visible, but there is no skin upon his thighs. The air is filled with falling strands of hair. Across the way, in the burned ruins of an inn, there remains only a stove, a bed, and a cellar door. A cauldron boils within the stove.

Go to the cauldron, tell what ye see inside.

I see . . . a melon covered with willow leaves. A dinner plate filled with red meat. The red becomes gray. The meat dries. Now cornstalks. Now stones.

Oh! That noise! A splitting sound. The leg of the bed has split. A crack appears in the door. I open the door and follow it to the basement. A crystal globe awaits. I stare into it. Behold:

A flying bird leaves him. Misfortune. The wild goose draws near the shore. It alights in the tree and begins to moult. Below, there is tethered a yellow cow and a gelded boar with but a single tusk. There should also be a goat; I am certain of this. But the goat has been lost. They drink from a magic pool.

A crane calls from the shade. I pull at ribbon grass and mulberry shoots. I climb the hill to eat the golden apples but only bare trees await me there. Thorns and thistles. A withered poplar.

Above the trees there is a lake. White rushes are spread underneath to soften the ground so that nothing should break. The lake takes fire yet the white of the rushes becomes hoarfrost. Solid ice is not far off, despite the fire.

Sand is near the bank. The water means danger. The flying bird brings a message: it is well to remain below. Polestars appear at noon. There is a broken jug near to the well. I go to the well and peer within. Only blackness below. I lean forward and the masonry crumbles at my touch.

I fall, I fall.

I fall.

Into the well.

Willan watched Hoxa's hands while the two men placed chessmen onto the board. Warlord and virgin, priest, paladin, and palace (sometimes called the rook), the metal figures left Hoxa's grip for their appointed squares. The hands were strong and without blemish. No dirt beneath the nails, no stains or inkspots, Hoxa's hands were those of a man who lived by speech, with few material records; a man who could rise to triumph from nowhere or be blotted from human memory with little effort.

Hoxa smiled. "As guest, the first move goes to you."

Willan moved a rook's pawn two squares. Hoxa raised an eyebrow.

"An unusual opening," said Hoxa.

Willan shrugged. "There is a theory to the effect that atypical strategies find strength through an opponent's unfamiliarity with their weaknesses."

An odd expression passed over Hoxa's face. "Very well then," he said. He moved a paladin from behind the row of pawns. "Let us strive for originality." Willan advanced his rook.

The game enveloped them. Time stretched and shrank with the intensity of concentration. At the tenth move, Hoxa said abstractedly, "Your show this evening was indeed a delight. But as an aficionado I must ask: How did you accomplish the last trick?"

"The rings?" said Willan, trying to maintain an air of detachment, though his ring finger tingled forcefully. "There is a small gap in some of the rings. The gap is hidden by the hands."

Hoxa shook his head. "I know of the basic ring trick. I could follow the gapped rings. But there was no gap in any of the last three; I was watching for it."

Willan said nothing for a moment, then moved his priest to threaten a pawn. "I confess that there was a small formulation of true magic in the last sequence," he said. "It was illusion only," he lied. "A flimsy bit of mass hypnosis to produce the appearance of a ring."

"I am sure that I would have penetrated any such illusion," said Hoxa, "unless your magical skills are much greater than any in this land." Hoxa's manner was offhand, but there was peril underneath. He moved a pawn.

Willan smiled blandly. "The other part of showmanship is misdirection. You were doubtless too intent upon the center ring. That ring was real. The two outer rings were illusory."

Hoxa scowled, doubt flickering behind his eyes.

From the head of the circle in the dim dark room Nara said, "Where are you?"

Young Aloquere replied, "I do not know. I am lost and I am cold, so cold. I stand in mud that bleeds. There is no sound, yet the wind howls."

"What do ye see?"

"I . . . I am afraid of this. It is vast. The world is vast. I see a flickering plain. There is pale lightning but no thunder. I see . . . a frown. A frown of light. The frowning mouth has teeth, fangs. Eight of them . . . no, seven. There is a gap where an eighth should be. There is an ache where the eighth should be. The song is broken and only shards of melody may be played."

"Where is the eight?"

"Low. Deep. Beyond the mist. The frown may not penetrate its own mist. It sits high in the clouds of despair and brokenness.

"Unity may only be found in hell. And then the hell may grow. I do not like this place. Please help me!" She sounded like a small girl.

"Come back," said Nara. "All is well. We are here. Ye may return."

"But wait!" said Aloquere with a note of wonder in her voice. "There is more about this place. The silent howling. The voices . . . They speak to the void. They speak to me as well. They are trying to . . . They are striving for . . . No. They cannot strive. They . . ." Her voice trailed off. She seemed to be listening.

"Return," said Nara. "Do not listen to the voices. They are past yer concern. Come back into the light."

"But they call to me," Aloquere said. "They wish to tell me of the things beyond knowing or caring." She listened once more. She said in wonder and sudden surprise, "Why, of course. Now I understand. It is because these people are all dead." The man seated next to her gave a nervous giggle.

"Quiet!" snapped Nara at the sound of the laughter. Then she said urgently, "Aloquere, listen to me. Return. Follow the sound of my voice. There is no fair converse between the living and the dead. Ye must not tarry in that place. Ye must not listen to the dead, only harm may come of it. Please come back."

"Pardon me, sir," said Aloquere, not listening to the dark witch, but to some other, alien sound. Her voice was now dreamy and soft. She said, "I seem to have become lost, perhaps I fell asleep. I am looking for my child, who passed this way before, I think. Many years ago. Have you seen her? Is there news?"

She gasped and shook herself and for a second her eyes darted about in panic. She shivered and cried out, her grip tightening upon the hands of her companions.

"Oh! Who are you? I believe we've met. Yes, I . . . No! Stay back. I did not want . . . I never . . . Oh! Oh!"

Her face contorted and she sat up very straight, then continued the motion until her back was painfully arched. She convulsed.

"Hold her!" commanded Ṇara. "Retain the circle; hold her tightly!"

Aloquere thrashed from side to side, moaning. The men on either side of her looked wildly about the circle of guests, uncertain and afraid.

She gasped and arched her back again, and a hot sensation passed from hand to hand about the circle. Fingers twitched. To harsh intake of breath and bulging eyes, a nimbus formed about the table. There were squeals and yelps.

Someone relinquished his grasp.

The pain of release was a physical blow. Several persons cried out. Aloquere overturned her chair and fell writhing to the floor. Nara leaped to her feet, but by the time she could round the table, Aloquere knelt glaring at the crowd of onlookers who stood against the wall. Her eyes were feral, her mouth a snarl.

Aloquere said, in a growl that was deep and harsh and hollow, "The murderers make merry, and why not? My grave is still warm, with plenty of fine meat for ghouls. But mind the poison in my flesh! There is enough to kill more than one." And the voice was a man's voice.

"Who are you?" said someone in fright, someone who had perhaps recognized the voice.

"I was Seilung!" snarled the voice within the girl. "But I am Seilung no more, for I was foully murdered and laid to keep but not to rest. And now I am vengeance!"

With those words Aloquere leaped, so suddenly that all were transfixed. A knife flashed within her grasp and at the last instant, Tilwesser the King threw up his arms to ward off the stab. The white of his sleeve turned red and he gasped in surprise and fear.

In the next instant Aloquere was dead at his feet, the sword of a guard doing its tardy work.

A woman screamed.

Chapter Twenty

Willan unobtrusively wiped his hands upon his legs. His palms were damp. The room felt hot, but his feet were cold.

His entire hand throbbed with his heartbeat and the ring upon his finger.

Hoxa had changed with the playing of the game. In some fashion he had lost possession of himself with the passing moves and a new personality had joined the game, bringing with it a style of play unlike any that Willan had ever seen. The attack came with darting movements of paladins and a slow surge of pawns. The strategies upon the board grew progressively more brilliant and bizarre.

The game had turned; Willan was losing.

The wizard felt an urge to hysterical laughter rise within him. He fought it down with effort. His predicament coiled about his mind and he did not dare give in to a full consideration of his circumstances. There was danger here, deadly danger, yet he must play chess. Indeed, the game was his defense. He had piqued his opponent's curiosity. Something malign had engaged with him for sport and a very good sport he must provide. A clever move on Willan's part and Hoxa would bend intently over the table. The sense of danger would become more distant as the alien will became engrossed. A temporary respite, then the presence would grow in power as Hoxa constructed a slashing edifice upon the chessboard. The checkered field held a vortex of strategy that grew inexorably as Willan's pieces were forced to retreat.

In the center were the horsemen, grinning and insane.

The paladins were perhaps the oldest of chess pieces, as if the first draught from the well of human invention had contained a recognition of madness. They traversed the board to their appointed positions without concourse on any intervening squares. They weaved in their attack: two steps forward, one to the side, one forward, then the two. They moved like snakes. Eight threatened squares straddled from a center point, they held like spiders.

Once, during the madness in the years that followed the Demon War, the paladins had been eliminated from the game by edict of the King. It was held that strategies involving the pieces were tinged with witchcraft, that necromantic lore was enciphered into the patterns of their movement. For a time chessmasters had met and played true chess like priests of a banned religion.

"Check," said Hoxa, his voice expressionless.

Willan surveyed the situation. Virgin and Warlord were threatened. To save them required the sacrifice of a priest. He reached to make the move.

There came a scream from far away, so distant as to be nearly inaudible.

The two men looked at each other. Hoxa's face slid into blankness. He seemed to be listening. Then a grimace of hate seized his features.

"Fool!" rasped Hoxa. "What have you . . . ?"

D'tias leaped to full length in Willan's grasp and he struck with a continuation of the motion. The flat struck Hoxa at the temple. The impact was more than the swing would justify. A shock numbed Willan's hand and the band upon his wrist glowed scarlet and silver. Hoxa fell, his eyes rolling up into his head.

Willan stood frozen for a moment, uncertain and wary. Should he slay Hoxa, or would the death give freedom to his adversary? Where was the Demon now?

There came another scream.

Willan bolted from the room, wrapping the shadows about him as he ran.

Tilwesser held his arm, his eyes bulging, his tunic spattered with blood, his own and Aloquere's. He turned and stared at Nara, now alone in the middle of the room.

"Sieze her!" commanded the King. With bloody hand he pointed at Britar across the ring of tables. "Him, too," he said.

Two guards advanced toward Nara. She stepped back and held up her hands, fingers moving. From across the room her staff leaped toward her, twisting as it flew. It caught the two men squarely in that place at the base of the skull. They fell like stones. Her staff sank into her grip.

A young soldier had drawn his sword upon Britar. The thief overturned a table, catching him at the ankles. There came a crunching of splintered wood and bone and Britar caught the soldier's sword as the man fell. In the next instant he slashed across the stomach of a nobleman who had come with dagger drawn to aid the soldier. The nobleman fell with a moan and the rest of the trysting pressed back against the wall or leaped for cover beneath the tables.

The remaining three of the King's bodyguards were joined by two other soldiers to rush upon Nara. They reached the center of the room and Nara made a cutting with one hand. The chandelier ropes parted. It fell with a flickering crash upon her attackers. Most of the remaining candles went out and the room filled with the smoke of wax. The walls took on an eerie flicker, now lit only by torchlight from the halls and a few last pitiful candles glowing above the broken bodies beneath them.

The King had fled to safety in the hall and more soldiers crowded to the door in answer to his shrieked commands. They gaped in dismay at the scene which confronted them: the huge short man with the bloody sword; the woman, dark as fear, standing before the bodies of the King's guards.

"Not another step," said Nara in clear forbidding tones. "Or I'll melt yer flesh with lightning. I'll turn yer bones to ash."

Britar's steady eyes took in the room. *We are lost*, he thought. *No other exits and we confront a host. If nothing else they can bury us in bodies or drown us in their blood.*

"Attack!" screamed the King. "Kill them now! Or I'll slit your cowardly throats myself!"

The mass of men, weapons drawn, swarmed through the door and rushed across the room.

And died.

The shadows rippled and became alive. A piercing shaft of light stabbed from the darkness. Like a spark in a fire-draught it darted from the depths and flickered over the band of men. Thus they died. By two, by four, blood spilling to the floor, fear striking to their souls, they faltered in their rush, and the deathlight, the sharp edge of radiance that was D'tias in a wizard's grasp, sliced their lives away.

Willan spoke from shadow. "Nara! Behind you, the wall! It is only brick and mortar, not stone."

Nara whirled and with a few long strides was at the wall, Britar close behind her. She swung her staff and a sunburst of cracks appeared upon the plaster covering the wall. Again she struck and with a *crunch* and a shower of brick, a hole yawned before them. Nara and Britar fled through it into the halls beyond.

They ran through the Palace halls with the speed of the general alarm. Most that they met were astonished at the sight of the running pair and the erupting din behind them and so gave wide passage. A few drew weapons and died before knowing the reason.

"Willan . . ." said Britar breathlessly as they ran.

"Later," spat Nara. "He'll join us later. He now slows the pursuit."

They ran into the courtyard adjoining the outer Palace walls. In front of them was the alley leading to the gates; beside them were the King's stables, housing the only horses allowed within the city.

"The horses . . ." began Britar, and again she plucked the thought from his mouth.

"No," she said. "Not worth the time." She swung her staff and smashed the wheel of a cart containing bales of hay. It toppled, spilling the bales onto the paving stones. She swung again and a bale burst its bindings. "Across the alleyway," she gasped.

Taking her intent, Britar lifted bales and hurled them from the cart. They formed a barricade across the narrow street behind them. Nara scraped her staff across the pavement and a shower of sparks kindled the hay into a blazing barrier. From within the Palace sounds of pursuit came to the pair as they ran through the gates into the Carnival night.

The crowded rhythm of the streets engulfed them, swallowing them up in snaking dances and throbbing parades.

Was there ever before a Carnival such as this? With such frenzied abandon, such desperate gaiety, such a denial of all tomorrows and the terrors that they may bring? The thunder of the music merged with the pounding in Britar's head and he thought he heard the call of madness. The dance drums spoke to him of war and chaos; he saw the landscape smeared with blood, though it was only torchlight, save for the scarlet upon his sword.

He pulled back his lips and forced his face into a hideous grin, a rictus of black humor. "Smile, laugh!" he called to his companion. "It's Carnival!"

Nara understood. Chameleon-like her manner changed and the pair of them merged with the frenzied gaiety of the crowds. They ceased to exist as single entities fleeing for their lives. They became as drops of blood, flowing through the Carnival Beast, for a time free of destiny and pursuit.

Through the wide spiraling streets, through the parks and past the palaces and temples, past the counting houses, past the factories, granaries, warehouses and slums they ran. Through littered streets and alleyways that stank of garbage they ran. And further.

Down to the waterfront. The smell of water came to them and Britar heard the sound of creaking docks. A locked gate appeared before them, Nara's staff touched ground and she vaulted over the neck-high fence without breaking stride. Britar leaped and hoisted himself to the top of the barrier, but his arms threatened to give as he tried to scramble over. There came a wavering in the shadows beneath him and Willan appeared, boosting Britar over the top. The big man landed heavily on the other side. Willan seemed to melt up and over the obstacle and then he was standing beside the panting thief.

"Thanks," gasped Britar.

"Come," said Willan, and he pulled his friend down to where Nara waited in a small boat.

They severed the mooring line and Britar looked around.

"Oars?" he said, though he expected none. Oars were not left waiting to be stolen.

"No," said Nara. She thrust her staff into the river behind the boat. The water churned. The boat leaped forward into the night.

Britar sank down to the hull and fell into a trance of reaction and fatigue. The night had overpowered him. He trembled and tried not to moan.

"Macou," he whispered. "O, Macou."

Part Three:

The Chaos Harp

Chapter Twenty-One

They traveled upstream through most of the night. Shortly before daybreak they came ashore and sank the boat behind them. They then stole horses from a demesne alongside the river. At Nara's insistence Willan burned the stable to obscure the theft.

They traveled overland for a time, toward the east, then hid for the remainder of the day beneath a rock formation at the center of a fallow field.

"We should have killed the King," said Nara while they rested. "The confusion would have hindered pursuit and could perhaps have delayed the war. Now both will be effected with the utmost urgency."

"We will be taken for Haldorian spies and assassins," said Willan. "The search for us will concentrate to the west. We should slip through unless Quecora manages to locate us and alerts his henchmen."

"Hah!" muttered Nara. "Why should he bother? We've done him nothing but favors so far. We've added fuel to the fires of war, worsened the intrigue in the court of R'tha, and even handed him another stone to cast at the gypsies. With adversaries such as we, he'll need few allies."

Willan looked at her. "Did we not snatch a geis from him and escape with our lives?" he said reprovingly. "I had hoped for no more."

Nara's face showed lines of strain. She sighed and nodded. "What ye say is true. We escaped with more than I'd dared hope. I will examine the geis when I am less tired, but I think that it is fruitful."

She sighed again and shook her head slowly from side to side. She stole a look at Britar, who seemed to be asleep. "The innocent pay the price for the guilty," she said. "I am so tired. I must rest, but I can only think of Aloquere and a man that I killed in the Palace halls because I thought he reached for his dagger. Now I am not even sure that he had one, just that he blocked my way."

They slept away the afternoon and most of the night. Dawn found Nara crosslegged on the ground, a pattern of pebbles in front of her, her eyes on distant places. Britar still slept a troubled sleep in the growing light and Willan observed them both as his dreams drained from him.

Presently the gypsy blinked and her attention returned to the physical world. She arose yawning and stretching and walked over to reseat herself by Willan. She spoke quietly to avoid disturbing Britar.

"The geis is strong and clear. Questions will be answered in the manner of oracles, which is to say that a geis is as trustworthy as any truthful madman. I have ascertained that we move in the proper direction. Our goal is to the east. Part of the vision is of a high place, shrouded and obscured. I believe they refer to the Mountains of Misfortune which separate eastern R'thern from the wastes beyond."

She described the vision of the geis to the wizard, the broken frown and the unfinished misty hells suggested by poor Aloquere. "Have ye any notion of these things?" she asked of the magician.

Willan nodded slowly. He said, "If the gap-toothed frown could be said to represent an arch with columns descending from it, then the object of our quest might be a Chaos Harp."

Nara looked at him blankly. She shook her head. "I have not heard of this device," she said.

"There is little information about it, even in the most arcane and fragmentary of Toltan historical texts. The most complete reference speaks of a class of devices called 'numerological engines,' of which the Harp of Chaos is the most powerful. The only other numerological device which is known is a simple toy called a 'dice rigger.' That one is misnamed actually; its appearance is similar to a tuning fork, and it can control the outcome of the roll of a single gambling cube. A pair of dice is beyond its power."

"It can control the workings of chance, then?" inquired Nara.

Willan nodded. "The power of a numerological engine is expressed in something called 'permutivity,' although the exact methods of calculation are based upon a mathematics which has fallen into obscurity, along with all knowledge of the construction of the more powerful engines.

"The Chaos Harp was a tool of the Demon and it was far more powerful than any similar human construct. I cannot even guess at its power when whole; such devices were used in the Southern War against the force of an entire race of wizards. If one survives . . ." Willan's voice trailed off as he became lost in thought. At length he spoke again.

"If a Chaos Harp survives, it cannot be intact, or at its full powers. If it were, Quecora would not bother to plot and scheme, he could have his way with the certitude of fate and the appearance of accident. The missing tooth must mean that a string of the Harp is missing. An incomplete numerological engine drastically loses permutivity. A dice rigger with an injured prong can barely affect a coin flip."

"Then ye think he tries to render his weapon whole," said Nara.

Willan nodded once more. "I am certain of it. We must deny him his goal. His grasp upon the world is still tenuous. It may slip. The monster might be thwarted by human perversity if nothing else. But with the forces of destiny at his whim . . . his grip becomes a stranglehold."

The sleeping Britar gave a groan and the gypsy glanced in his direction. His dreams, she knew, were of his falcon, caged and helpless, decorating some contemptible patrician dwelling. Or starving to submission for some nobleman's sport.

But fortune smiled upon the unhappy thief that day. When he awoke Britar said nothing of Macou. He helped

to prepare the meal which they ate before resuming their
journey. He made tactical comments concerning their escape
and route of retreat. He listened with full attention to his
companions' explanations of the new direction of their quest.
And if he brooded, he hid his preoccupation. His inner mood
could be guessed only from the way in which he gazed at the
last of the summer dust devils as they danced upon the arid
land around them. The dusty whirlpools floated free above
the dryness which thirsted for the autumn rains. He felt a kinship to that which thirsted. But he did not complain.

It happened that the trio was discussing the tryst ghost of
old Seilung and the message that he brought.

"Did Tilwesser kill the old King?" asked Britar. "Seilung's
ghost left that impression."

"There is no reason to believe that death confers infallibility," said Nara. "Even if one believes that it was really Seilung
that appeared and not some group creation of capricious
spirit, why trust either his opinions or his truthfulness?"

"There are many possible explanations for the events
which occurred at the trysting," said Willan. "Only a few of
these require that Tilwesser actually slew his father."

"Perhaps so," said Britar. "But may the truth be unraveled?
Certainly the simplest explanation is that Tilwesser is responsible for the deed."

Willan nodded. "Seilung was murdered; that much is certain. It does seem plausible that Tilwesser had a hand toward
the deed. He may find it necessary to have a scapegoat."

"He will use us for that purpose," said Nara. "I am inclined
to the belief that . . ." Her voice trailed off and her attention
slid upward.

"What is it?" Willan asked.

"I am not sure," said Nara. She hesitated, weighing the
dangers of false hope. At last she said, "I think that it might
be Macou."

Britar jerked in his saddle. "Where?" he gasped, frantically
scanning the skies.

"There," said Nara, pointing to a place in the blue expanse
above them where imagination, if delirious or suggestible,
might place a speck just at the edge of sight.

Britar brought his fingers to his mouth and cast forth a piercing whistle into the sky.

Slowly, very slowly, for the distances involved were large, the speck became a flying creature and the creature became Macou. Britar wrapped a cloth about his arm and held it up as a perch for the rapidly diving bird. A flurry of wing and happy screeching landed upon Britar's arm and the two engaged in a flutter and a frenzy of odd whistles and caresses that made the reunion comical in its affection.

"Macou! Macou!" jabbered Britar happily. "You found me!"

"When ye did not return to pay for the falcon's boarding, the keeper must have released him," said Nara.

"More likely he tried to put Macou in a cage or tried to put a hood on him," said Willan.

"No matter," said Britar, his face broad and smiling. "Macou escaped to find me again. That is what matters. It is a miracle of good fortune."

"Best to enjoy it then," Willan said. "We may not get many more."

Beyond the floodplain of the Yes, water grows too scarce and unreliable for agriculture. Farming is replaced by the ranching of cattle and an occasional tended herd of goats. In the dry season, as grass grows scarce, even the goats draw toward the west. Travel toward the east finds a landscape progressively more barren until only a thin cover of dry grass holds the desert at bay and the only inhabitants are the stray animals that crowd around the water holes.

The trio now made swift travel. They had no longer any need for stealth, and while the region was severe of climate, they had no difficulty locating what water there was. From on high Macou could see for miles to lead them to the patches of faded green surrounding surface water. Nara's Sight could even trace subterranean rivers as they meandered near the surface. Food was as easily acquired as water, since to find one was to find the other.

Nara's curiosity had been piqued by the return of Macou. She wondered if there might be some psychic link between

Britar and his pet and if this meant that Britar possessed talents similar to her own. Willan expressed doubts. He thought it more likely that the bird had found them through search and the keen vision of a predator. Moreover, if talent existed, only something akin to wizard's speech was indicated. The Sight was a rarer skill and unrelated. He, himself, had heard his father's death over a hundred leagues span, yet the Sight was not in him at all.

Despite Willan's opinions Nara contrived to test Britar's ability. She had him assume the crosslegged position of meditation and bade him gaze upon pebble patterns that she constructed. She instructed him in the inner quiet necessary for an unleashing of the clear white light. The results were less than satisfactory.

"No," she told him. "Ye must not allow sensation to distract ye. Placid mind, calm breath. Drift."

"But my legs hurt," Britar complained.

"No, they do not. There is no damage to them. Yer legs are uncomfortable. Yer mind mistakes this for pain. Control the mind. The illusions will vanish."

"That is easy for you to say. Yer joints are as flexible as rope. Mine creak and groan. It certainly feels like pain to me."

"Look," she said still another time. "The legs are crossed to feed the brain with blood and to help cast free the soul. It is a poor freedom that requires perfect comfort. Concentrate. Ignore yer surroundings."

Britar tried for a while longer. Nara at last shook her head and bade him unlace his body. He did so and gave a sigh of relief.

She said, "Ye may have a bit of the Sight, but we shall probably never know. It requires a peculiar discipline to control. Ye do not have the inner nature required to unlock the talent if talent ye possess. Ye are correct in the judgment that my own is a different case. I have no choice in the matter. I must control the talent or it would swallow me." She sighed.

"I am sorry," Britar said. "I wish that I could be better."

"It is no reflection upon ye or upon yer worthiness," she said. "The discipline is hard and with little reward. Indeed, the idea of reward is foreign to it. The one question that prophecy cannot ever answer is 'How do I get what I want?' One may find money—if one does not care for wealth. One may seek water—if one can ignore one's thirst.

"The desirous question is doubly proscribed. Firstly, it is ambiguous. It points to fancy, not fact. Its attainment would be subjective at best, impossible at worst. Secondly, the desire itself clouds the vision. Desire makes the Sight perverse. To want something pushes it away."

Britar inquired, "Is there then not a paradox in our present position? We are here as a result of your abilities after all. We follow your vision to attain a goal."

Nara replied with a touch of irony, "I have missed something, I think. Did any of us want to be here?" She indicated the surroundings.

"The geis which we follow is an enigma, a dream requiring interpretation. Our need to avoid Quecora made it so. We do need the means of his defeat. We do not have this nor will my Sight provide it. The geis merely keeps us in the game. Whether we win or lose, or even whether our actions help or hinder our cause, these things are wholly upon our heads. We have no assurances. We must trust to our courage and the purity of our intentions."

Britar appeared to be slightly taken aback. He asked, "Do you mean that we might be unwittingly aiding our adversary?" When she nodded he thought for a minute, then said, "The gift of prophecy does not seem very useful, then."

She said, "Have I ever claimed that it was a desirable thing, this 'gift' of mine? Am I rich, well-loved, admired because of it? Do any envy my position? Would a citizen of R'tha trade places with me, if given the opportunity? Does Haldor lay honors at my feet?"

Her voice became urgent. "If the Sight is a boon," she asked, "why does it wane with each passing generation? If prophecy is a noble state, *why am I the last?*"

Chapter Twenty-Two

The landscape grew uneven as they traversed the eastern plains. They had turned northeast and once more they encountered the thin high clouds that presaged the winter rains. The terrain began to rise and fall gently. At the crest of one of the small hills Nara said that she caught a glimpse of mountains in the distance.

Days passed and the features of their surroundings grew more emphatic. The roll of the hills grew in height. The clouds above them became thick and gray. From time to time a stand of stunted trees appeared.

Willan watched Macou fly high overhead. He scowled. There was something about the sight of the falcon that bothered him. Or perhaps not the sight itself, but the words that might be used to describe the bird in flight. Floating on the breeze. Hovering on the wind. Sailing on the . . . He shook his head. There was a taste of uneasiness in his mind. He felt as if he were trying to remember something that he had forgotten long ago. Something about . . .

As he watched Macou shifted in his flight and began a double circle overhead. In the same instant Willan's ring began its warning tingle.

"Willan . . ." Britar began.

"I know," the wizard said.

The hill in front of them held a scattering of trees, several of which had been killed by thorns. From behind a tree at the top of the hill stepped a figure in armor. The metal was shiny black. The figure drew a sword as black as the armor which enwrapped him and waited for their approach.

Willan hesitated, weighing possibilities. He sensed power; flight would merely postpone the battle and would perhaps give the black knight time to gather allies. What . . .

Willan felt a flow in the air, emanating from behind him. He turned to see Nara with her staff held high, weaving a spell of power.

"No, wait!" he called to her, but it was too late.

The coiling spell which the gyspy loosed made contact with the armored one. He swung his sword and cut to the center of it with contemptuous ease. The force of the spell unraveled and a backlash surged at the trio.

Both Nara and her horse collapsed instantly and fell heavily to the ground. Nara pitched free and lay still. Britar, less sensitive and farther removed from the backlash, fought for consciousness but finally succumbed and slumped forward in his saddle as his horse fell. The band upon Willan's wrist glowed a sooty color as the power washed over him. He leaped to the ground, D'tias at full length, and approached his foe.

The first contact was nearly death for the tall wizard. The black figure moved with a speed which one would presume impossible for one encumbered with armor. A flash of darkness, a thrusting cut clumsily parried, and the black sword slashed over Willan's ribs. Pain erupted with the blood, the hurt overlaid with the sparkling agony of magic as the band on Willan's wrist glowed gold and scarlet with the deepness of the wound. Despair sliced through the magician worse than any sword cut, for he knew the figure in black to be far the superior swordsman. The pain sent Willan's mind curling inward upon itself as he prepared to die.

Ironically, this may have saved him. For when his mind abandoned hope his body slipped free, and D'tias moved to some will other than his own, to thrust and parry its ebon-bladed adversary like a thing alive. Willan's sword flickered and snapped to block the dark attack and at each singing *clang* there were sparks and the impact of sorcery nullified.

A strange thing now came to Willan, his body and soul divided into motion and pain. A third part of the wizard now waked, as if from a deep slumber, and began to assess his plight. There was no pain or fear to this new consciousness, only a calm calculation tinged with curious purpose.

His adversary moved with inhuman perfection; only the power of D'tias held the black sword at bay. And Willan's inner self perceived this to be only a temporary respite, for D'tias would surely fail when the flesh and bone that grasped it collapsed with fatigue.

And even if he should be able to penetrate the fine classicism of the black knight's swordsmanship, there was the swart armor of his foe. The few brief touches which D'tias made drew sparking jolts but no damage, not even a mar upon the midnight sheen. Not so the armored one's frequent violations of Willan's person. These had resulted in minor cuts save for the first, but they did find blood and they burned with the hint of hell.

Willan gave ground as the first glimmering of a plan came to him. His wrist grew black and shadow swirled about him like the fog. The creature before him was a thing of shadow also, he realized, and the battle must be won in the territory of the night.

Eil, cut, *sweil*, thrust, *dreid*, parry and return. Over, *fura*, under *sunf*, slash, and yield and turn. The two figures now were shimmering phantoms, lost in the twilight of perception. There rose a wind from nowhere, with the sound of a deathlaugh shaking through the bare trees around them.

The dark one is perfect, the shadows whispered to him. Like a textbook recitation of an ancient spell, crystalline, inflexible, brittle. Unsurpassed within the framework of his existence: sword against sword, swordsman against swordsman. You'll find no flaw that will yield to a direct assault.

Willan's foot slipped upon a rock and the dark one was upon him in an instant, nearly finding the pathway to his heart. The wizard twisted frantically, and parried the thrust with his left arm. The black sword cut his forearm and shoulder deeply. Willan retreated rapidly, his back now nearly against the trunk of a corpselike tree. Blood flowed freely down his arm, yet the pain no longer added to his fear. His inner self was merging with his soul and body once again and his previous animal terror began to drain away.

Break the rules, the whisper came to him. Abandon swordsmanship and training. Smash this machine which threatens you.

Giddiness overwhelmed him and he laughed out loud as he pointed to the sky with a bloody hand. The dark foe ignored him and began a pattern of attack. Willan seemed to slip again, then fell sideways as the ebon thrust began. His ring flashed and a tree branch overhead exploded into flame, falling, catching the dark figure at the wrist and driving the black sword into the ground.

D'tias became a dagger in Willan's hand, black with the shadows, dark as the figure before him. He thrust. Into the black armor went his blade. Through the black metal and a dagger of darkness became a sword of light.

The impact and transformation rattled Willan's teeth. His wrist band flared a blinding white as both man and sword were hurled sideways to the ground. A sparking hole appeared in the black swordsman's side. The armor quivered, shook. A fine green powder ran from the wound, evaporating as it fell. The air filled with an overpowering stench. The armor collapsed.

As Willian watched, the metal armor went from black to gray. Then the first spots of rust appeared. The brown corrosion spread, and metal flakes began to fall. The hole which Willan had made grew rapidly with the rusting to reveal the interior of the armor. The armor was hollow now.

After only a few minutes the dissolution was complete. Nothing remained but powdered rust, blowing in the wind, joining the smoke from the burning tree limb. Willan waved his arm and the fire went out. Then he went to tend to his wounds and those of his companions.

Chapter Twenty-Three

In the days that followed Nara became withdrawn, seldom speaking unless in response, seldom smiling for any reason. Each night found her staring for hours into the dying camp-fire; each dawn found her in the attitude of prophecy, crosslegged and intent upon the pebble patterns at her feet.

The two men left her to her mood. They knew her well enough by now to know that any attempt to draw her out would be fruitless. Indeed, they could easily guess at her concerns. She had miscalculated in the affair with the black swordsman. She had seen no vision of his arrival, no harbingers of his power. What other hidden dangers lay before them? What other misread futures lay in store?

For her own part Nara battled doubt as she examined and reexamined the net which she had cast about their fate. Try as she might she could obtain no glimmer of the figure in black armor. That fish had escaped her forever. She did not dare cast her net again; the waters held the leviathan, the Beast named Demon. So she brooded over the patterns and her doubts multiplied like the fishes.

The travelers left the desert floor and climbed the small range of hills that formed the western side of Kunado, the last valley. Kunado was lush and green, pleasant contrast to the desert which they had left. Far to the south the valley merged with the desert once more when the river of Kunado reached Salt Lake. But this far north the valley still tapped the northern mists, the winter rains, and the glaciers high in the mountains at Kunado's eastern edge.

To the east of Kunado was the edge of the world, the Mountains of Misfortune. Beyond them lay the Abyss.

The Mountains were impenetrable by land. Some geographies survived from before the War, when magical flight was still possible and the Abyss had first been crudely mapped from above. The descriptions told of great fissures in the earth, from which erupted acrid gases and lava flows. They told of a ragged landscape, of great chunks of the earth's crust thrown up and tilting, like jagged ice floes in a thaw. They told of giant mountains so high that there was still ice upon them even though they burned with volcanic fire. And they told of rains and mist so sour that rock dissolved into blowing red powder that colored everything the color of blood, both the unliving soil and that which tried to grow in it. There was a saying: "Beyond the edge of the world, even the ground bleeds."

So the trio came down from the hills into the valley at the edge of the world.

A sudden rainfall had swelled a small creek and this they followed until it reached the River of Kunado. The river was not wide at this point; they found an easy fording only a few leagues to the north and they crossed over. A short distance on the other side they came to the main road which ran north-south through the entirety of Kunado. It was here that Nara's divinations became completely perverse.

The gypsy stared at the geis patterns for hours, stretching her Sight to its limits. From time to time she would reach out and shift a pebble in the pattern. Nothing availed. Finally she arose and kicked the rocks into a jumble, swearing forcefully.

"Nothing works!" she exclaimed. "Retreat is pointless. To the South lies disaster. To the North lies death and the East shows only an unclimbable rock cliff. All our options seem either useless or suicidal. But the complexity of the geis hints at other things as well. I am baffled. I have never seen such a jumbled fate."

"Perhaps we should wait here for a time," suggested the wizard. "The time may not be right for movement."

She shook her head. "When patience is counseled, the signs are clear. We are not urged to inaction. Quite the contrary, the situation is urgent and something must be done. But what? We can stay here until we starve to death, but that would not help our cause."

"Should we split up, then?" asked Britar.

For a moment Nara seemed startled. Then she scowled. "I had not thought of that," she said. She returned to her place and arrayed the geis pattern once again. Once more her presence slipped into the void.

After many long minutes her eyes refocused, though her voice remained soft and whispery and she did not move her position. "Ye are correct," she said. "We must divide our forces. I overlooked that possibility and allowed my attention to become fixed upon the three of us as a group. I had assumed that I would have to guide all of us to our goal. It seems that I was mistaken. Now why . . . ?" She stared into the spaces beyond the pattern before her. "Ah," she said at length. "It does not pay to consider oneself to be indispensible." She smiled and climbed to her feet.

"Ye must memorize the geis pattern," she told Willan. "Our paths diverge. Ye are to take the road to the north while Britar and I go south. There is a camp of gypsies but a day or two north of here. There is one in that camp who can read a geis and who can give to ye any advice concerning the final pathway to yer goal. Here." She handed him a disk of metal, a coin or a medallion from an ancient time. "Give this in payment to the one ye find there. She will know from whom it comes. And she will not dare to tell ye anything but the truth."

She went to the horses and began to rearrange their few remaining provisions. Willan and Britar moved to help her. Nara shook her head and pointed to Willan and the geis pattern. "Britar and I will do the repacking," she said. "Ye must memorize the pattern. We have wasted too much time here already."

They remained camped for several hours, until Nara had assured herself that Willan could accurately reproduce the geis pattern and several of its variations. They then made plans to reunite along the road after the completion of their tasks, whatever these might prove to be, assuming success and survival. They made no plans for failure. Death would take care of its own.

The leave-taking was brief. Then Willan turned his horse

to the north while Nara and Britar rode south.

The gypsy and the thief said little for a time, each trying privately to digest this new turn of events. Macou perched upon Britar's shoulder and from time to time the man would stroke the falcon's head. Finally Britar spoke.

"Why do you think our fate requires two paths?" he asked. "It seems to me that separation greatly reduces our strength."

"I agree," said Nara. "Surely it was the desire to remain as a group that so jumbled my reading of the geis. Our three sets of abilities blend very well. I regret this, but the fortunes cannot be denied. We search for two objects: the Harp of Chaos and its missing string. I daresay Willan is on the path to the one; we search for the other. I do not know which one is to be our prize. Nor do I know why we must seek out both objects simultaneously.

"All yer questions will have answers soon, I think. Our fate draws very near."

They camped for the night and resumed travel at first light. By noon they had traveled far enough to the south to again see blue skies before them. To their left, the great cliffs had given way to numerous canyons and hills with scrub forest cover. Occasionally they saw a solitary tended field. Macou took to the air and spent the early afternoon playing amongst the patchy clouds overhead.

They were tired and thirsty when they came to the village. The daytime light had many hours yet to shine but they decided to stop and rest. They would eat at the inn and quench their thirst. Then they would decide when to resume their travel. The inn had ample accommodations, though it was small, for there were fewer visitors than rooms. They might spend the night there and perhaps obtain useful information from other guests.

The village itself was small; aside from the inn and its attached tavern there was only a smith's and a general merchandiser with a livestock yard in the back. High on the hill behind the inn there stood a house. It came to Nara that the next nearest habitation was in the valley beyond that hill.

Overall, the scene was lethargic. A few locals were transacting business or fleeing farm chores with a drink or two at the tavern. The surrounding countryside gave evidence of only desultory agriculture. An occasional traveler from the north or west might reach this place, but most of those present came from no farther than a few leagues to the south. There were few people in sight, perhaps a dozen including those inspecting livestock in the yard.

Nara and Britar sat at a table on the tavern porch and sipped from their mugs of ale—against all etiquette, which says that the beverage should be quaffed. In such a lonely place it was difficult to feel strongly about etiquette. Indeed, it was difficult to feel strongly about anything, despite the urgency of their mission. There was something languid about the mood of their surroundings, the slow clouds overhead, the soft voices of rustic conversation, the smell of water and growing grass.

Suddenly, there came to Nara a feeling of tension and unease. Britar took the feeling from her, as a consequence of their widening rapport. She spoke to him in a whisper none but he could hear and which scarcely moved her lips.

"Do ye feel that? It is a collective. All of these people here, they are now thinking of the same thing, though they try not to show it."

Britar nodded and returned her whisper, "What is the cause?"

"I do not . . ." she began. "No, wait, there. Over there. That old woman walking with the young boy. The villagers are all trying not to look at her."

The pair which Nara mentioned were walking down the street toward the store and livestock yard. They were still some thirty yards distant, but their path would bring them in front of the inn, where the horses were tethered. The woman was old in appearance, with deep lines in her forehead and white hair only occasionally showing a dark streak of its original color. The boy with her was quite young, perhaps four or five years old. Dark-eyed and shy, he clutched at the woman's skirts as if she were his mother, though to look at them, child and grandmother was more likely.

"Let us tend to our horses," said Nara with impulsive curiosity. "They will pass near enough for me to read."

The gypsy and the thief arose from their table and crossed over the porch to the railing where they had tied their mounts. Britar fumbled with his horse's bags and Nara stepped back from him just as the old woman and child ap-

proached. It seemed an accidental encounter, Nara lightly.
brushing the woman's shawl just as she passed by. And
then . . .

Down.

Into another's world.

*He came to me in winter, when the trees were stripped bare
and the blackness of night seemed an eternity. The light hung
about him like spring and with it he banished the coldness
from my dreams. He was the sun itself; I melted before his radiance. He inhaled my substance like a rare scent. He molded
me; my poor worthless clay became sculpture to his touch.
Though he has gone, I am his vessel still. My arms still remember his embrace. My loins still smolder from his caress. I
am his chalice, his serving cup.*

*His child is mine; so great a blessing he left to me. Oh, the
power of his seed and its result, our offspring, has drained
me, consumed me. Yes it is true. The child has tasted blood
with mother's milk. No matter. Were the child to drain my
very soul, I would offer it gladly. He is my soul. He is my existence. I am old while still the child is young. No matter. I
will die before the child is grown. No matter. I am shunned
and outcast. No matter. My task is fulfilled. Our child lives
and grows. Our love will live and grow.*

I would repeat the deed a thousand times.

Nara reeled. She stumbled forward, clutching at Britar's
arm. He heard her voice, clear, urgent, and unspoken. "Brit,
help me! Keep her from me. Get me out of here!"

Britar stepped between Nara and the woman with her
child. "Is anything the matter?" the woman said, in a voice
that was not old at all. "Is your friend all right?"

"She is given to fainting spells," said Britar smoothly. "She
will be fine very soon." He lifted Nara onto her horse where
she clutched the animal's neck, trying not to let her body
shake.

The old-young woman looked at Nara and scowled. "I
suppose that you know best," she said dubiously. Her son
looked bewildered and tightened his grip upon her skirt. She
stroked his hair absently. "Come, Rako," she said. "We must
see the shopkeeper." The pair turned and walked away.

Britar guided Nara's horse as they rode away from the
town. When they had passed from its sight Britar asked,

"What happened? Are you becoming ill?"

She shook her head. "Did ye not hear her voice? She is not old. She has barely twenty-five years of age. She was Quecora's consort once. Her son is the Demon's child."

Britar's forehead wrinkled as he shook his head in disbelief. "But how is that possible?" he asked.

"The Demon may possess a human body or take on human form. It does not matter which, the result would be the same. The child was born out of wedlock. That is why mother and child are shunned. That and superstitious fear of her fate, her appearance. If those peasants but knew . . . They would burn her, I think. They would kill the child."

Britar thought for a moment. "Should that not be done? Should progeny of the Demon be allowed to live?"

She looked at him. Sadness grew within her and seemed to fill her to the brim. "Are we now so desperate that we must murder children? Are we so sure of our justice that even love must be snuffed out? The child is a product of love, Brit; he cannot be wholly evil. The woman was Quecora's willing consort. She has paid her price; must her child pay as well?"

Britar's lips grew thin and tight, a troubled look alighting upon his face. After many long minutes of silence he blurted, "But she could not have known with whom she . . ." He stopped again, then said, "Why did she do it?"

Nara looked around her at the unchanging hills, through eyes that knew another's memories. She saw the stifling grayness that underlay the languid peace. One could travel for days and not see more than a score of people, each no different from the last. She saw the chains which bound the villagers to their land. She saw the past merge with the present to extinguish the future. "She did it for love," she told her companion. "He was the grandest thing that she had ever seen. She did it for love."

Chapter Twenty-Four

The rain had only just ended when Willan rode into the gyspy camp. Mud clung to the hooves of his horse. Water still pooled in the ruts made by the gypsy wagons' wheels. It reflected the gray sky and the many-colored cloths of the tents in the camp. Cooking fires filled the air with smoke and the smells of stewing meat. Willan's mouth watered and his stomach growled. Off to his left, the sound of dripping rainwater mingled with the restless shuffle of animals trying to keep warm in the damp.

Most of the gypsies ignored him. An exception was an adolescent girl who looked up at him flirtatiously as she leaned over to stir a boiling stew pot. Behind her, an older man glared as the wizard rode past. Willan did not let his attention linger. Whoever they were, daughter, father, sister, brother, husband, wife (he knew so little of gypsies), he wanted no trouble.

He came to a man who sat on a stool carving a wooden figure with a shining knife. Willan stopped his horse and waited. Nothing about the seated man changed, except for his attention.

"I have a need," said Willan.

The man continued to carve. "And who does not?" he replied.

"I will pay to see mine satisfied," said Willan.

The gypsy ceased carving but remained silent.

"I have a fate that needs reading," continued Willan.

The man resumed his carving. "The black tent houses the witch," he said.

"Thank you," said Willan. He turned his horse toward the black tent. He flipped a coin behind him to the ground beside the man on the stool. The coin remained untouched until Willan had gone.

The door flap of the black tent was closed. Willan dismounted and clapped his hands sharply. "Hello, inside," he said in a voice that was neither loud nor soft.

"What do ye want?" came the rasping response.

"To come inside, for first," replied Willan.

"Very well, then. I cannot stop ye."

Willan pulled back the flap and stooped to enter the tent. The stale air from within caught him full in the face, full of old food aromas and the pungency of wine. Overriding all else was the smell of ganja and numbsmoke. Nara had told him that many gypsy seers required drugs to bring forth their Sight and the gnarled black woman he now confronted would seem to be one of these.

She sat crosslegged on the ground, a low table in front of her. The table contained a few remaining crumbs of a meal, a bottle of wine and an incense burner. A smoky candle stood off to one side, providing the only light within the tent. The woman looked at Willan with large-pupiled eyes, while her hands turned cards from a deck, one after another.

"Ye are inside," she said. "Anything more will cost ye."

Willan reached into his pouch and removed the coin which Nara had given him. He handed it to the woman and said, "I've a geis which I want you to read for me."

She looked at the coin and her lips moved slightly, forming a sneer. He wondered if she were going to spit at him. Instead, she turned away and said to herself in a low mutter, "So the iron virgin still lives. A pity." Her voice became louder. She looked at Willan. "I'd have thought her dead long ago. Her sort calls up their own destruction; don't need the Sight to know the truth to that. Still, if the dark bitch lives and commands a favor, is it my place to refuse? Not mine to stop a fate. Best to get on with it, let ye find yer deaths quickly so the rest of us can sleep peacefully . . ." Her voice faded and her attention slipped away for several seconds. Then her eyes refocused. She said, "Well, what are ye waiting for? Let me see the geis."

Willan pulled a handful of pebbles from his pouch and carefully arranged them on the table. A curve of eight stones, then three above and five below. A seemingly random scatter on both sides, then he placed two stones, touching, near the center of the eight stones of the arch.

"There it lies," he said.

The gypsy reached beneath the table and grabbed a handful of leaves and dried flower petals from a hidden bowl. She tossed the handful into the incense burner where a hot coal ignited and thick smoke plumed forth. She leaned over the bowl and breathed deeply.

The smoke made Willan's head swim. He tried not to breathe it in but it seeped into his nostrils and tickled his throat. He squinted his eyes to try to pierce the haze before him as the candle's glow became fuzzy and indistinct. The tightness in his arm and shoulder lessened, the faint ache left the scars remaining from his recent wounds.

He wondered at this woman and the hatred which she carried for Nara. He wondered if the woman could be trusted. What had Nara done to inspire such rancor? Within the haze which filled the tent, only her voice came to him with clarity.

The gypsy mumbled a bit in a little singsong. Then her eyes opened wide. "Aha!" she said excitedly, an odd look of dispassion and curiosity on her face. "So that is why this place seemed so serene. The eye of the storm." She giggled in a parody of girlish laughter. "Marl will be annoyed. We shall have to move when the storm breaks."

She looked at Willan. The smoke had smoothed the hard edges from her face. She almost smiled. "This is a very dangerous geis," she said in a chatty tone. "Ye are in it and ye have no sense, so ye will not heed my advice. But I say 'give it up.' Some fates are better left unfilled."

"I search for a prize," said Willan, still trying not to breathe too deeply of the smoke which gave visions and blotted out all pain. "Tell me where I may find it."

She waved her hand in an airy gesture. "High up," she said.

"Near to water and ice. Ye seek a mountain. We would be in that mountain's shadow if shadows pierced the clouds. Ride east a bit. The trail up the mountain runs north-northeast." She gave him a look that from a younger woman might have been meant to be alluring. From her, it seemed either ironic or contemptuous. She laughed a low laugh at his impassive expression. She seemed to be enjoying a joke at his expense.

"Go on," she said. "It is as I say. Ye may trust my words. East, then north. Yer prize awaits. Stop in to see me when ye return from yer glorious fate."

She leaned back onto a pillow and began to laugh uncontrollably. "Glorious fate," she said. "Ha, ha, ha. Such a colorful phrase. Glorious fate. It fairly rings! Be sure to see me when it is finished with ye."

Willan arose and left the tent. Her laughter followed him.

Nara read the pebbles for the last time in the crimson of late afternoon. The clouds overhead glowed pink and orange and even the grass looked sunburned. The geis read clear and sharp. No ambiguity remained. Turn east, it said. Climb. Follow the light into the darkness and descend into the earth.

"Well?" asked Britar as Nara scooped up the stones and replaced them in her pouch.

"Well," stated the gypsy as she rose and walked over to her horse, "it will not be long now." On an impulse she opened her pouch again and removed five coins. She tossed them to the ground and stared intently at the result.

"What do they say?" asked Britar, who was becoming impatient to leave.

" 'When there are no choices there can be no blame,' " Nara quoted from an ancient text. " 'All must pass through the gate.' " She climbed onto her horse and pointed toward the east. "Our destination is not far from here. We will be there soon."

Britar continued to look at the coins. "What gate?" he asked, his impatience ebbing from him. "What is the meaning of the coins?"

"They tell us that we are beyond the point where questions matter. Get up on yer horse."

"Don't you want your coins?" he asked.

"No," she replied.

The last rays of sunlight lit the entrance to the mountains' labyrinths. Macou swooped down to alight upon Britar's shoulder as they entered, and clung tightly to Britar's shoulder as he followed Nara downward through the narrow passageways into the caverns below the mountains. The witch's staff shed a soft light that made the damp stone walls glisten with their passage.

"Macou does not like this place," said Britar, wincing at the sharpness of the falcon's talons upon his shoulder. "I am not fond of it myself. If we lose our way, we will have a ready tomb."

"Hush," said Nara. "That is the least of our worries. There is something . . ."

She stopped and reached out to touch the nearest stone wall. She stepped back and the light from her staff went out. But instead of darkness, there remained a pearly light which seeped from scattered patches in the rock.

"Glowstone," she said. "That explains why Quecora could not find the prize that awaits us. Willan has told me that the Chaos Harp is constructed of material similar in composition to glowstone. I think we search for the missing string and that someone long ago hid it very well."

They continued downward. Britar kept silent, but he thought constantly of the mass of earth which hung above their heads. He barked his shin upon an outcropping as they turned around a bend. Then they ducked beneath a low archway and, suddenly, they stood in a chamber.

The cavern was enormous, high roofed and as large as a city square. It glowed, with great luminescent stalactites forming chandeliers far overhead. The sound of dripping water, multiplied by a thousand echoes, whirled around them like insect chirrups. A slight smell of brimstone touched their nostrils from the air that came to them from deep underground.

"Oh," said Nara, taken by surprise. She had known the cavern was here, but knowledge and experience are different things.

"Macou!" hissed Britar, the bird taking wing from his shoulder. "We are not outside. There is no game here. Come back!" But the falcon's flight arched high across the chamber, flirting with the stalactites and circling as if searching for something.

"Leave him," said Nara. "We must search for the Chaos Harp. Over there." She pointed to a recess in a far wall. The stone in that area was more iridescent even than the rock overhead. The pair hurried toward the glow. As they approached, they saw that a niche had been carved in the stone of the cavern wall. Within the niche was a green glowing rod of stone.

But when Nara and Britar had reached a dozen paces from the string of the broken Chaos Harp, Macou swooped down to light beside the niche. There came a shriek from the bird which transfixed the gypsy and the thief, and then the cry was cut short. A blur surrounded the figure of Macou, a kaleidoscope mist that made vision slide past and the eyes refuse to focus. The blur grew and the falcon was lost within it. Another figure appeared, indistinct and ambiguous. It might have been a man, or perhaps not. But the figure held up an arm (or something like an arm) and a voice echoed through the chamber.

"Weight!" it said admonishingly, and then there came a giggle in another voice.

In the next moment Britar felt as if a giant's hand had landed upon his back. He fought, but it crushed him down. He could no longer breathe. Beside him he heard a moan as Nara too fell beneath the sudden increase in gravity and her staff clattered from her grasp.

The ground was very hard. But they felt it only briefly before darkness claimed them.

Chapter Twenty-Five

After only a short climb Willan and his horse pierced the clouds which hung low upon the landscape. The going was easy enough. There was a pathway up the mountain, though the trail was nearly overgrown and showed no signs of recent use. It wound back and forth and around the hillside, sometimes even descending briefly before resuming the ascent. The grade seldom became steep enough to force Willan to dismount. The greatest hardship of the climb was the boredom and gray sameness of the fog-enshrouded scenery.

Willan yawned and stretched in his saddle. Rumblings from his stomach reminded him that he had not eaten since early morning. What time was it? He could not judge the sun through the fog, but it must be afternoon. His horse had become sluggish, perhaps with weariness. Willan dismounted and unslung his pack.

The meal was unsatisfying. His food lacked savor and he found that he had scant appetite despite his stomach pangs. His horse also was slow in eating. The meal took longer than Willan expected and he began to wonder if he would reach his goal by nightfall. The thought did not disturb him. He repacked and mounted his horse.

The grade became steeper and rocks began to litter his path. His horse's sluggishness had perversely increased after their stopping. Periodically Willan had to urge his mount onward, first with words, then with slaps to the rump. Willan's annoyance with the animal grew.

The air was damp with the fog, though not uncomfortably cold. The landscape, what he could see of it, seemed peaceful and serene. Occasionally he heard the sound of trickling water from a brook and the scurryings of small animals. One could live on this mountain for a time even without provisions, he thought. Game must be plentiful if men avoided the mountain, as seemed to be the case.

Eventually there came a time when his efforts no longer sufficed and his animal would no longer move despite his urgings. Willan spoke a few profanities, then dismounted. Whence came the horse's stubbornness? His ring should have told him of any magical hindrances. Was there subtlety too great to trigger the warning? Or was the animal simply willful or ailing? He cast his perceptions into the fog. The taste of magic came to him, but weakly. Perhaps it was imagination. No threat surely.

With a scowl, Willan dismounted and removed provisions from his bags. The horse stood still, its eyes dull and apathetic. With a gesture of annoyance the wizard turned and began to climb.

His anger at his circumstances faded as he climbed. The path steepened and became more irregular. Soon he was moving through terrain which might have been dangerous to travel on horseback. There would be too great a chance of a misstep. There was no great loss, he decided. He would be on foot by now anyway. And the path was still not hard to travel, just rocky and uneven. It was still not steep enough to cause him to sweat.

The gray closed in about him more thickly. The foggy curtain seemed almost pleasant in its uniformity. A certain laxity seeped into his limbs.

Would he reach the summit by nightfall? Probably not, but since his eyes could pierce the darkness it did not matter, except that it would become colder. He did not relish the thought of spending the night alone on the side of a mountain. Yet that was his prospect if he failed to reach his goal before fatigue overtook him. He realized that he knew neither the time it would take him to reach the summit, nor precisely how long he had been climbing. At least he would know when night fell.

Suppose his goal eluded him? There was no surety that this was the correct path, despite the gypsy's claims. Instinct assured him that he proceeded correctly, but he had been mistaken before. He winced at the recollection of some of his previous errors, the storm which had destroyed Nara's home, the affair in the town where he had met Britar, others prior to that, through the years too numerous to count. No, he mused, infallibility was not one of his traits.

Even if this were the path to either the imperfect Chaos Harp or its missing part, there was no certainty that he would be able to destroy it before his efforts came to the attention of the Demon. He might even be leading his adversary to the goal. The possibility made him shudder.

There came to Willan an image of the Demon laughing cruelly at his efforts, toying with him and snatching away victory just as it came within his grasp. For some reason this image then transmuted into a memory of his first days in Haldor, just after entering the University in Thile. His speech had been tinged with hill dialect and his manners had been crude and gawky, a far cry from the smooth and mysterious sorcerer he fancied himself. It had not taken him long to discover that magic was a crude tool and no substitute at all for worldly experience. Indeed, he had not dared to use his talents and he had soon found himself made sport of, taunted, teased, his affections trifled with. More than once he had suffered the cruel jests of the young women in that city. His cheeks burned at some of his recollections.

He shook his head as if to fling the thoughts from his head. What was the matter with him? Certainly he was no stranger to failure, but he had survived and persevered. And why dwell on petty matters? It annoyed him to think that his past embarrassments should impinge upon his consciousness at such a time. There was no comparison between previous hardships and his present situation. Could the memory of mocking laughter loom larger than the enslavement of the world?

As he pondered, the answer came to him that perhaps it could. The fate of the world was too large to hold in mind and one's emotions shied away from such an abyss of failure. So the fear seeped in around the edges of thought. And the fear became annoyance and uneasiness and even ennui. Was that it? Was it fear that fatigued him so?

His steps felt leaden and the fresh scars on his shoulder and forearm ached. He stopped to rest.

Where had all his efforts brought him? Risking death, or worse, in an attempt to hold back an avalanche. He strove for a purely negative goal: Quecora's defeat. The absence of one particular tyranny. Yet nothing would be solved by this outcome. Pain would continue; senseless death would still exist. War would certainly not vanish from the earth. The Demon merely exploited human weakness, he did not create it.

Willan thought, my father is dead, my heritage lost. I have had few friends and these I've abandoned at the dictates of my training and my quest. I am an outlaw in two lands, thought a spy and assassin by the two most powerful nations in the world. What is left for me but to continue with my climb?

He rose and began again to climb.

Night fell and wizard's light sprang up around him. The fog thickened and his world reduced to an expanse of but a few paces. He felt isolated and alone. He might as well be the only man in the world. Time began to slip past him like pebbles through nerveless fingers. He tried to count his paces but his attention kept drifting away. He recited poetry but the fog swallowed it up and his voice trailed off when he forgot the words. He stopped once more to rest and lost an indeterminate time to reverie and remembrance. It was so hard to marshal the effort to arise that he bit down hard upon his thumb to startle his mind and body to awareness. The bite drew blood and the pain energized him for a while. Then it joined with his other aches to throb dully and sap his will. He was afraid to stop again.

He told himself that he was under some sort of attack and this served to give him firmness for a while. But doubts nibbled away at this conjecture. What manner of aggression was this? He felt no danger, merely discouragement and fatigue. His pains were no worse than could be explained by the damp and cold. And why no warning from his ring? Could his present path be merely a blind alley, a useless pursuit, with only disappointment at the summit? This now seemed a likely possibility to him. But how to explain his inner turmoil and lack of resolve? Why was it so hard to continue to put one foot in front of another?

Or was this really new to him? How firm were his inner forces? He had followed his father's wishes until Vitor's death, then he had undertaken his quest at the direction of the Oracle of B'ru. Nara and her Sight had guided him until but a few days previous, and now, deprived of the will of others, he was unwinding like a clockwork toy. He had no obvious enemy to fight. He had no way to know if he would reach his goal, nor any way of knowing what he would do if he reached it. And if he were successful, if he smashed the Chaos Harp and defeated Quecora (unlikely possibilities), what then? He had no life to resume. No family. A wizard in a world where magic was dying.

His family had loved skill and competence above all else. His travels had been dictated by the ancient methodologies of Toltan education. Feed the body, feed the mind, feed the soul. Exercise one's talents. Discover the world. Return with the spoils of education: knowledge and techniques. Where other peoples searched after gold, his heritage searched for knowledge. Yet where did it end? With himself, last of the line, filled to the brim with decaying minutiae and worthless skills. All knowledge turned back on itself eventually and became superstition and error.

He sighed. His nostrils filled briefly with the scent of blithany, a delicate herb which grew in the melting snows of the mountains of his childhood. A pang of homesickness drifted through him and he inhaled deeply. The scent was gone. Only damp fog and the smell of grass and dew remained.

To where could he turn for sanctuary of the spirit? To thoughts of love? He thought of the women he had known and loved. Where were they now? His childhood sweetheart had married his brother Jephred when Willan had gone off to school. In Thile he had known two lovers, Tedith, the aristocrat who had used him for sport, playing up to him when it suited her, then turning cold when he came too close. Jorane had soothed his soul for a time and then had vanished with only a brief, unsatisfactory note of farewell. He had tried to follow her, but none would tell him where she had gone. Her image still haunted him on the glimpsed faces of serving girls and carriaged ladies.

There were others he remembered. He mourned them all. They danced before him as if to remind him of mortality. Di, the minor actress who had taken him to her room to show him her "breathing exercises," a euphemism for certain drugs of pleasure. The farmer's wife who seduced him during a storm and whose memory would have brought pleasure if he could only remember her name. Or the one named Mirane, who had cried after making love because he had been drunk when they had met and she knew that he would leave her.

He remembered the hurts and forgotten promises and wondered if any had a choice about the outcome of love and whether that outcome could be anything but pain. No, he would not be saved by love.

Nor would friendship succor him. Time and distance ate like acid at the bonds which tied him to those he remembered. His boyhood friends were strangers to him now. His best friends during his schooling, what had become of them? One was dead; two were married and fattening when last he saw them. He had lost touch with so many through the years.

And Mulau, the kind old man whose heart he had broken almost by accident, who had taken Willan as his apprentice only to discover, instead of an heir ("you are as a son to me"), a changeling. A wizard who partook of the learning and skills, but who would not carry on the craft.

And Nara and Britar. (Why did he think of them as dead?)

He stumbled forward. He thought of childhood dreams: all perished, dried up, abandoned. He took another step. He remembered adolescent love: melted like the snow. Another step. Youthful ambition: too grand for attainment. Daydreams and hope: folly and futility. Knowledge and craft: pedantry and rote. He took another step.

The wizard's light flickered whenever he blinked. It was an effort to breathe. The past confronted him. The future assailed him. The present bore down upon him like a heavy weight.

With a tremendous effort he took another lurching step, then he slipped upon a rock and fell headlong onto the cool, cool grass, wet with dew.

Chapter Twenty-Six

Near Haldor pass, the fog poured slowly from the hollows of the hills, like the exhalation of a sleeping god. As the fog descended, it merged with the dew and mist of the valley floor. Battle neared. All who breathed knew its scent. Above the hills the moon glowed scarlet, portent of the hell to come. The fog played hide and seek with the devil moon, covering it with clotted clouds in one moment, in the next parting to let the bloodlight spill through. From a lookout perch high upon a hill two sentries pass the time by matching coins.

"Horns," says one. "I win again."

"You win too much," says the other.

"You think I cheat?" rejoins the first. It is not a serious question. The men are friends, beyond cheating, and the first one, Roz, is known for his painful honesty besides.

"No, I do not think you a cheat," says his friend. He stands and stretches. "But I grow tired of this game. It worries me also, for reasons I cannot name."

"Because you lose," says Roz, with a smirk in his voice.

"Oh, all *right*," says the other and he kneels again. "Toss a coin."

They flip their coins and show the faces. Matched horns and Roz wins the other's coin. If crosses show, the fortune is reversed. No match is a draw. "Horns again," says Roz, and he scoops up his friend's coin.

"Enough!" says the other, whose name is Gil, and as if to punctuate his words, the moon slips behind a cloud. Gil stands and walks to the edge of the precipice and stares into the blackness below.

"How many is that?" he asks Roz. "How many tosses gave us horns?"

"Several dozen," says Roz. "Maybe two score."

"Does that not disturb you?" Gil asks.

"Why should it?" Roz replies. "I've been winning. I'll give you back your money if you wish."

Gil smiles viciously into the night. "It's not the money," he says. "It's . . ." He pauses, then starts again. "Gypsies believe that fates are foretold in the toss of the coins."

"Superstitions," says Roz. "You're sounding like an old woman. You should never have learned to read. It turns your mind to mush."

Gil is silent, his head moving from side to side, a nervous habit. Roz, afraid that he has given offense, opens his mouth to speak. Gil turns and cuts him off with a wave of his hand.

"No, wait," says Gil. "Hear me out. We wait for the sound of the attack. There will be a battle, yes? Two armies meet. Violence, bloodshed. Chaos rules. In the course of events, many things occur. Horses stumble—by chance. Swords slip—by chance. Eyes blink at the wrong instant, arrows are nudged by breezes, sweat runs into your eyes just as the enemy nears, all quite by accident and happenstance. And it evens out, yes? Neither side carries the day because all of the other horsemen fell into holes or because the wind's caprice blew their arrows from the mark. Chance plays no favorites, you see my point? Fate should not operate at so mundane a level."

"So?" says Roz.

"And coins should not turn horn side up *each* time they are tossed."

"I fail to see your point," says Roz. "Men are not coins, nor are horses or arrows." He observes the sky. "There now, the moon returns. Do you wish to continue?"

Gil hurls a coin at Roz's feet. Horns again. "Getting to be a bore then, is it?" asks Roz.

"Oh no," says Gil, his words mixing irony and sarcasm. "The suspense is terrible." He looks once more into the valley below. "Have you no fear?" he asks softly.

"Fear?"

"Fear!" snaps Gil in fury, flinging another coin to the ground. "The crack that might flood your brain with light!"

Roz draws back, then notices the coin upon the ground. Unable to resist, he flips another to a place beside it. Both horns for yet another time.

"I'm afraid that this isn't your day," says Roz.

"I'm afraid that it is," replies Gil.

Chapter Twenty-Seven

Britar of Freeland was conscious for many long minutes before he could think of anything beyond the force which pressed him to the ground and squeezed the breath from his body. Resistance was useless; it took all his will to feed his lungs with a trickle of air.

He heard voices. There seemed to be an ongoing dialogue and discussion concerning a fine point of theology, carried on by two voices which were emotionless and dust-dry. He could barely hear them; the words were so quiet. A third voice was much louder and there was a richness to it. It sang:

> I went to the devils' kitchen
> To get my food one morning
> And there I got souls piping hot
> That on the spit were turning,
> And still I sing bonny boys,
> Bonny mad boys,
> All my boys are bonny.
> They all go bare and they live by the air
> And they want no drink nor money.

Britar could not raise his head against the crushing pressure which held him, but he could turn his head slightly toward the sound. A shadowy figure stood a dozen yards away. Before the shadows floated the glowing string of the Chaos Harp. Around the string was a brighter glow, comprised of multicolored threads of light which warped and tangled one into another to form a loose fabric. The crystal shaft of the Chaos Harp was becoming encased by the light. The shadowed figure gestured periodically and another strand of radiance formed and weaved itself into the colorful mass.

Britar stared at the figure of Quecora the Demon and tried to see his form. He could not. His eyes refused to convey details. His gaze slid first to one side then another. He could make out no specifics of the entity which moved and sang and even debated with itself (Britar tried not to think how many mouths this implied). Quecora had bested them at every turn and he, Britar, could not even see his adversary.

Damn you, he thought savagely. *What have you done to Macou?*

The voice that was singing stopped and chuckled. "I have not harmed your pet," Quecora said. "I have only borrowed his substance for a while, to wrap about my own true form. There is not much bulk to a falcon, I am afraid, not enough to fashion a worthy persona for myself. I can barely provide a presence with this bird-cloak of mine and I dare not stretch it any more, lest it shred. That *would* harm the animal and give you a glimpse of my true form as well. You would find the latter quite as distasteful as the former, I assure you."

Quecora whistled a little melody and Britar thought that he heard one of the dry scholarly voices say, ". . . eternal recurrence . . ." But the discussion became inaudible once more. Several more bright threads joined that which Quecora wove.

"This will be done shortly," said the Demon. "Then to grander things. And what would you ask for your own new fate?"

Britar said nothing—but then, he could not.

"I rather like you," said Quecora, conversationally. "Some of it is probably contagion from the bird. I do take on certain qualities from those I mount. The bond between you and the one you call Macou is very strong. He might well have found you again after your little adventure in R'tha even without my assistance and the judicious use of my Chaos Harp. Though the Harp is damaged and greatly weakened, it was quite easy to reunite the two of you, so fate must have been on your side from the outset."

Quecora observed the look upon Britar's face as another thread was spun.

"You need not feel so betrayed," said the Demon. "I do have some rights by prior ownership, you know. Your pet is a windhover, a breed I myself created centuries ago. They were my spies, my messengers, sometimes even my mounts, though I had little need for such transportation then. Your friend Willan was about to remember the name 'windhover' when I arranged for a diversion. That puzzles me. How could the magician have remembered a name which he had never heard before, eh? Yet he nearly did remember and it cost me the black warrior, a loss I do begrudge. I do not like your friends as much as I like you, good thief. I might even say that I do not like them at all."

The Demon paused once more. The fabric of light about the Chaos string was complete. "No matter," said Quecora. "You friend Willan is truly of no consequence now. He breathes the vapors of despair and none ever escape from that fate. Besides, I have other tasks."

Quecora lifted his arms (were there only two?) and gave a cry. The light in front of him flashed and died. The crystal string had vanished. For the barest instant, Britar felt a lessening of the enormous weight which crushed him. Then it bore down again. Lying next to him, Nara gave a little moan.

Quecora sighed. "That was far more difficult than it should be. Once I would have taken it myself. Now all my actions are at a distance."

There appeared before him a rainbow arch of light, not the Chaos Harp itself, but a simulacrum. Quecora reached out and touched a spark of radiance. A sad sweet sound issued forth and drenched the world with color which echoed from the simulacrum to the Harp so many miles away and in the onlookers' minds long after the note had died.

"You see," said Quecora. "It works." Perhaps he smiled.

He stood before the fate of the world and stared into its face. His voice was no longer the friendly, chatty voice with which he had been speaking, nor was it the dry objective voice of scholarship or science. There was a deadness to this new oration that made one think of scar tissue and putrescence. He said:

"It is common among adolescents to wish for absolute control of the passions; some even aspire to disinterest and complete freedom from fleshy frailty. It is also a common fear of middle age that the youthful folly has been granted and that no desire remains, no lust, no will. The irony is there for any to discover.

"I was dead for a long time after my defeat, so many years ago. My kind does not sleep, so I am sure that it was death I felt. And yet I dreamed as if I had been asleep. I dreamed . . ." His form became still with the remembering.

"I dreamed things beyond comprehension. I dreamed worlds beyond knowing, each a different drama. I was participant in some of them, sometimes devil, sometimes god. More often I was of no consequence, a flea upon the back of fate. Passion ebbed from me as I dreamt. What is passion to a flea? I was dead for centuries. I grew to accept my own corpse. I was dead forever in my dreams.

"And then I dreamt I was devil to a world of magic and the forces of magic fell about me and were destroyed. And when I woke I found myself upon that world. And I had so small a power that it was a sand grain next to the boulder of my former self and still, *still*, I was the most powerful of all.

"And yet it remains dreamlike. Perhaps my kind do sleep and I am aslumber still. The times before this moment fade so easily . . ." He reached out and drew another melancholy note from the fates before him.

"However, it is amusing and I have no better game to play. How unfortunate for you! I think there are some passions still to kindle. If mine are cool, I'll rouse some heat in others."

The Demon reached his hand to the crystal fates and struck a chord. Its color was scarlet and its sound was War. The notes of Greed, Pride, and Fear echoed throughout the world.

From the chord of War he isolated the note of Pride and built upon it, leaving the others alone because those qualities grow so easily by themselves. To Pride he harmonized Patriotism and Valor, set to a march beat.

Beneath this sound of glory, way down deep in the bass notes of indigo and umber, where veniality lives, he plucked the strings of Ambition and Avarice. With these sounds he drew generals, merchants, all of the profiteers of war into the net of his new fate. He plucked the strings of Sacrifice and won tax assessors and clergy to his cause as well.

Quecora let the war tides build. They were already in motion; he fed their savagery with his skill. Then he began to weave a counterpoint. He struck another chord and this was Religion.

To a note of Piety he added Self-Righteousness, Faith, and Obedience. It added to the pattern well, sub-dominant to the war chord theme. As battle ebbed, religious ecstasy could grow. He sowed the seeds that would bear the fruit that mystics crave, the truths that allow no others dissonant to themselves.

And then a minor chord. First, disease. Plague and Pestilence. But not in a human key. The chord linked cats and rats and the trailing note was Famine, to draw tight the noose.

Then resolution. The tonic chord to seal the fate.

He rang the changes and modulations. From three basic harmonies he built a symphony. And these were the melodies he played:

The army of Haldor would be crushed in battle. The storm that followed battle would turn retreat to rout. R'thern would sustain only a few important casualties (a skeptic, a visionary, a clear-eyed observer of things as they really are, see them fall like the first ripe fruit, no longer to obstruct the wind's free flow). There would be tribute, there would be the fat years. The empire would grow, gorged on foreign wealth. The new religions would grow.

Then would come the pestilence, the famine, the lean years. A plague would strike the cats of R'tha and the rats would overrun the granaries. Another spasmodic war with a Haldor not yet recovered from the last conflict. R'thern would win, but there would be no spoils this time, for there would be no wealth to seize. Famine in both lands. Then turmoil, collapse, and civil war.

From the ashes would rise the theocracy, the first in centuries. There would be a new empire, ruled by the priests who paid homage to Quecora himself. All would be complete.

It was a mighty edifice, this Fate which the Demon constructed. Strong and glittering, it stretched into time as far as the mind could see. He fed its power. He hardened its structure. It grew to engulf the world.

He did not notice the mouse at its foundations.

He crawled. The rock and grit scraped his hands and belly. Tears of frustration leaked from his eyes and down his nose. His thoughts babbled in his ears.

The wizard thought, why do I hurt? I am the only thing in the universe. I *am* the universe. All is as I command, is it not?

The fire ring is a warning of danger. Yet how can it warn of human frailty? Of inner weakness? Is there a defense against memory? A cure for moral cowardice?

My death means nothing to anyone but me. My life means nothing to anyone but me. An arbitrary collection of moving meat becomes an arbitrary collection of decaying meat. No significance added or removed.

To be betrayed by philosophy, he thought. How strange.

A rock loomed in front of him. To his dull vision it seemed a boulder, a cliff, a mountain. There was no room to crawl around it. He reached up, pulled, clawed weakly for support. He managed to get his feet under him and he shoved with his legs. The rock scraped his chest as he managed to climb atop the obstacle. He rolled and fell to ground on the other side. His ankle throbbed. Had he sprained it earlier? Or just now? He could not tell. He had no strength for memory.

He lay with his head propped against the rock. The smell of brimstone came faintly to him. He knew that he should get up. He could not remember why. He knew that he should resume his crawling forward. It was too much effort.

He lay there for an eternity, placid and calm, steeped in the waters of despair. Slowly the fog began to melt away. He came to realize that he lay at the shore of a mountain lake. Above was the glacier that crouched on the mountain peak. He could climb no higher.

A slight breeze brushed by, bringing with it vapors from the lake. They stank of sulphur and rotting egg. A glimmering came to the corner of his eye. After a long moment his head rolled toward the light, almost as if he had willed it.

The alabaster arch stood before him like a broken frown. Seven columns descended from the device, like teeth, a jagged gap in the middle where an eighth would be. Firefly lights danced over the columns. He heard soft voices call.

As he watched, there came a glowing to the gap, a fine sparkling mist. The mist condensed and the gap was filled. The Chaos Harp was whole.

There was a sound and a feeling of change. The first string of the Harp glowed red. The second became orange, the third yellow, then through the scale to indigo. The lights began to move and dance and new colors formed which he could not name and which hurt his eyes. A new low sound began, which prickled his skin and made his head ache. He seemed to hear the voice of a teacher, an uncle long since dead. A voice from a dream. And the dream said:

"Mortal man sees cause and effect where only happenstance prevails."

"Reality is chaos underlying a thin veneer of order. From blind occurrence weak man extracts a fragile structure. Mere coincidence he calls natural law."

"*Chaos Harp* is but one name. *Numerological engine* is another. It acts upon the timeless moment between possibility and actuality, its power limited solely by the combinations possible to adjoining 'strings,' the crystal shafts hanging from its cycloid arch. Eight columns from the harp entire. With the fourth one missing, the power merely whispers. With the engine divided into three and four, it offers but a dozen dozen future paths. Enough to control a game of dice, perhaps, but not the lives of men.

"But if the Harp be whole, beware. Its power flows from two to four to six and eight. Over thirty-five myriad possible events does it reach. Twenty-five hundred times its broken strength. Its power will not whisper but shout. Bellow. Roar!

"It will rend the fabric of the times. Mold them to *one* dread desire."

Willan slowly rolled to his belly. He began to crawl.

And his mind said:

"You might still escape. It is within your power. Turn and flee. You have battled upstream; 'tis easy to return and good speed, too."

Of course, he replied and continued further.

His despair said:

"They are dead, your friends. Dead, or they have betrayed you. The proof is before you. They lost their prize. They were no stronger than you. They, too, fall and are dust."

Most probably, he assented and continued forward.

And his heart said:

"It is all for naught. You will expend yourself and die and

still Quecora will win. Or not win. It does not matter. All you loved is worthless ashes. Your knowledge is lies. The ages will roll and your death is nothing."

Well, of course, he replied.

He pulled himself upright on a pile of rocks. His lips curled. It might have been a smile.

You outwit yourselves, my weaknesses. If all is ashes, what matters my pain? All things are equal; it is mine to choose. I choose death; and it is mine to choose the manner and time.

He took a stance before the keystone of the arch.

I choose now, in malice and spite. They are all that are left me. They are enough. If I am a dead man, I shall have my revenge.

He raised his sword high above the Harp of Chaos. All around him was a mighty structure, a cathedral of Fate, built to an alien god. He now confronted that god. And he said aloud:

"I know you, Quecora, as you know me. We were made for each other. I am the embodiment of your destruction as you are mine. We are each other's deaths.

"I choose now," he repeated.

The Demon cried, *"No!"*

But it was too late. The sword swung. The Harp of Chaos shattered and Fate's foundations turned to sand.

Error erupted. Heresy prevailed. Happenstance tottered sideways and wobbled on its axis. The future slipped askew. Quecora's mighty edifice trembled.

The Demon set himself and heaved, and the structure righted itself momentarily. He could not save his vision of power, yet still he must stop the power from destroying the vision in its entirety. He might still salvage something. Quecora set himself counter to the runaway forces which thrashed around him and threatened to destroy all his plans. He braced himself and gave another shove. More power spilled and splashed about him like a flame.

The pressure upon the bodies of Nara and Britar vacillated wildly. One moment it lessened. In the next it crushed them until the darkness grew. Britar fought and raised himself an inch, then was slammed to the ground with bruising force.

"Brit! My staff!" gasped Nara.

She was pinned, straining, her fingers inches from the shaft of wood. Britar gathered himself and lifted. He scraped forward painfully, garments and the skin beneath shredding against the hard stone floor. Again. Another lurching scrape. His fingers closed around the gypsy's staff. He twisted his wrist. The staff reached Nara's outstretched fingers.

At the gypsy's touch the shaft of wood leaped. It lanced through the air and stabbed into the Demon's form.

Quecora screamed.

The staff exploded into splinters, unleashing forces finding focus there. But the sound of the shattering wood was drowned out by the agony of Quecora's wail. It was a death scream, loud enough to tear a hole in time. Beneath its final echoes, the rattle of a titan's death, came a rumble from deep underground.

And Quecora died.

The ground shakes . . . .

In Thieves' Waste a man clutches his breast and falls. He dies. He is found later, no marks upon him save for a curious burn over his heart beneath a hidden pouch. The pouch contains only worthless lumps of quartz.

. . . the earth quakes . . .

In R'tha, a bureaucrat named Hoxa, sequestered behind locked doors, pauses in the midst of an incantation. He finds that he can no longer remember how the syllables should sound. He scowls. He rises and steps over to consult a text. Its pages now are blank.

. . . he clutches at the rock floor, trying for purchase . . .

Three acolytes enter the temple of the Old God Who Is Now Renewed. It is silent. They call to the priest. The silence remains. They enter the inner chambers. The priest lies dead, his throat cut by his own hand, his blood congealing upon the altar stone.

. . . stalactites rattle overhead . . .

A timber snaps and breaks. The roof collapses. With a bellow of dust and belching smoke, the bloodstone mine caves in to bury what is now tons of worthless mineral far underground.

. . . spears of rock fall all around . . .

Storm clouds swirl over the mountains, hours too soon. The battle between the armies of Haldor and R'thern wallows in a sea of mud. Discipline collapses as nearby rivers overflow their banks and flood the battlefield. Both sides flee.

    . . . shattering glowstone flashes through the chamber . . .

Lightning from a cloudless sky stabs down to kill a noble of the court of R'tha, advisor to the new King, and his companion. His companion is found to be a spy. The King reacts in fear and orders the deaths of two other men, friends of the dead man. Thus begins a terror that will result in many more accusations, executions, and murders. The King himself will die less than a year later. Some will say from poison, others will know it to be from fear.

    . . . as the wind from beneath the earth rises to a frightful howl.

And then it was over.

The earthquake had not lasted long. Nor was there much fallen rock, billowing dust or acrid fumes as such things go. Yet when the shivering ceased, Britar opened his eyes to look around in surprise. He had expected to die. He could scarcely believe that the world still existed.

He raised his head and climbed to his hands and knees. He began to crawl toward the spot where Quecora had stood. The thief's clothing hung in tatters. His face and chest had been scraped raw. The floor was littered with wooden slivers and splinters of stone which ground into his knees and hands. He did not notice any of these things.

Where Quecora had stood the stone was dry. The dampness had been scorched from it. It was here that Britar found the crumpled body of Macou. The man sat down beside the bird and stroked the singed and broken feathered body. He wept.

Epilog

Where have you been?
Where no one knows.
Where are you bound?
Where magic goes.

The children were singing and jumping rope when they saw the strangers. They ran to tell their parents. The people of the village met the travelers and made them welcome.

There was something about the three of them that caused the village folk to speak of them in whispers. The whispers were not simply the hushed tones that one uses when discussing the sick, though one of them had been gravely ill when he arrived, tied to a pallet pulled behind a horse. He was very slow in recovering as well. Some of the village women thought him apoplectic; certainly he gave the appearance of one so stricken, his right side nearly paralyzed, his speech when it finally returned being full of halts and misspoken words. But his right arm was even more withered than one would expect, and one of the old women who had nursed him for a while spoke of a terrible scar upon his hand, as if he had tightly grasped red hot metal until it scorched the bone.

There was also an air about the three of them, a sense of wisdom and sadness and other things which confused the villagers and made them doubtful of their own knowledge of the world.

The visitors were given all that they required, which was

little enough. Food and firewood, a small stone hut on a hill at the edge of town. Old witch-women came from the surrounding countryside to aid in the care of the stricken one. Young village girls did their best to cheer the second man, the short burly one who grieved, though for whom or what he would not say. The young men brought him ale.

The tall black woman with the golden eyes was often seen at night, wandering the fields and hills, to what purpose none could guess.

Britar left the small hut and gently closed the door behind him. Nara waited for him by the fence in front. "How does he fare?" she asked.

"He is sleeping now," Britar replied. "I told him that I was leaving and we talked until he grew tired. He gave me this." Britar showed to her a small lump of metal that had once been part of Willan's sword, D'tias. It was fused and blackened. Piercing its center was a sliver of blond wood, a remnant of Nara's shattered staff.

Nara caressed the splinter. "So far to travel," she murmured. She stroked the metal with a searching touch. "No magic left," she said softly. Then she said more clearly, "I wish that ye did not have to go."

Britar said, "The days are heavy on me here. I need some silence for a while and then some city babble. But I will return. Someone has said that only thieves and gypsies speak ill of returning to where one has once been. I think my thieving days are past. I will be back."

Nara smiled at him, then the smile faded as she looked past him to the hut where Willan slept. "If ever I was gypsy, I am gypsy no longer. I will stay here."

"Will he recover?" asked Britar.

"I do not know," she said truthfully. "I have lost my Sight of things yet to be. I have gazed on too much naked fate and it has blinded me. Now I think my dreams are wholly mine, untainted by the destinies of men or the workings of the world. Life seems oddly flat with private dreams." Her voice was slightly wistful.

She looked again at the hut. "I think that he will get better," she said. "I believe this to be so. His strength slowly returns. He will probably walk again, though he may never run. We all paid dearly, didn't we, Brit? Ye lost Macou and I my Sight and staff. But he paid the highest price."

He took her hand in his and held it for a long time, looking into her face as she tried to hold back the tears. Then they embraced, almost convulsively, clutching at each other as desperately as two survivors from a storm at sea. There was laughter along with the weeping, and she brushed his cheek with her hand and brought his tears to her own face to mingle with the salt already upon her cheeks. And she hugged him to her once again.

She said, "Oh, Brit, such a story that ye have to sing, so fantastic that none will believe it."

And he spoke, smiling and hoarse. "They will if I sing loudly enough," he said.